POWER SPELLS FOR TEENS

POWER SPELLS FOR TEENS

ALYRA

CITADEL PRESS
Kensington Publishing Corp.
www.kensingtonbooks.com

Read and use this book at your own risk. The author accepts no responsibility for use and misuse of materials and processes in this book. All fire, including burning candles and incense, is dangerous. Every fire should be attended to at all times. Some of the materials listed in this book are composed of naturally occurring toxins and poisons. Do not ingest items not sold for eating. Take great care with all items.

CITADEL PRESS BOOKS are published by

Kensington Publishing Corp.
850 Third Avenue
New York, NY 10022

All Kensington titles, imprints, and distributed lines are available at special quantity discounts for bulk purchases for sales promotions, premiums, fund-raising, educational, or institutional use. Special book excerpts or customized printings can also be created to fit specific needs. For details, write or phone the office of the Kensington special sales manager: Kensington Publishing Corp., 850 Third Avenue, New York, NY 10022, attn: Special Sales Department; phone 1-800-221-2647.

CITADEL PRESS and the Citadel logo are Reg. U.S. Pat. & TM Off.

First printing: September 2005

10 9 8 7 6 5 4 3 2 1

Printed in the United States of America

Library of Congress Control Number: 2005922710

ISBN 0-8065-2599-1

For A. L. C.

C⊕NTENTS

ACKNOWLEDGMENTS

THANKS TO Mom and Dad. Thanks to K and G. Thanks to Elizabeth for helping me through "massage" class. Thanks to RR who made time and space for me to write this, to S who might read it someday, and to Jo who thought the process of writing would never end. Thanks to my readers A, C, K, and L for invaluable insight.

Special thanks to my editor, Bob Shuman, who encouraged me from the beginning and guided me through the process.

Thanks to Bonnie Fredman for her eagle eye in copyediting. Thanks to Kristine Noble-Mills for a knockout cover. Thanks to Anne Ricigliano of Planet Patti for the book's accessible interior design. Thanks to Arthur Maisel for his expertise in moving the book through production.

POWER SPELLS FOR TEENS

INTRODUCTION

I CAST MY FIRST SPELL when I was nine years old after reading a fantasy book. I thought that casting a spell sounded like fun, so I tried it. I asked for what I wanted most at that time, which was piano lessons. On a winter day I drew a picture of a piano on a piece of paper, wrapped it around a stick, and tossed it in my fireplace to burn. To my surprise, shortly thereafter my parents agreed to sign me up for piano lessons. They bought a piano, albeit secondhand, but still, it was a huge musical instrument in our house just for me! I played it joyfully for a year, and then I began to loathe practicing. I have not turned into a concert pianist, and the piano is gone having been sold thirdhand to someone else. But since that time I have become an adept spellcaster. Spells were my first experience with *magick*, and because of that piano, I proved to myself that magick is real and that spells work.

I'm not going to say that I also didn't tell my parents that I wanted to play the piano because I probably did, but that doesn't mean the spell didn't work. I asked for many different things, and my parents didn't get all those things for me. They did, however, get the piano, and that was what I'd cast the spell for.

Since that time, I cast a spell to get my prom dress when no store seemed to carry my size in the dress I had to have, and of course I got it. At one time I needed prescription drugs for my cramps each month, but now I don't. These changes didn't happen overnight. But they happened, and I caused them by casting spells. And so can you. I'm not promising that your parents will buy you a piano. I don't expect that you want a piano, but whatever you want, you can effectively use spells to help you get it. Spells are the first experience with magick that most of us have. And I suspect that you'll like casting spells and develop a life-long interest in magick.

If you do, you will change. That is akin to saying that "you will die some day" because we will all die eventually and everyone changes all the time. But I'm talking about big changes, the kinds of changes that you make to alter your entire life. Decisions such as what do you want to do for a career, where do you want to live, and what kind of person do you want to be. Most of us let the process of life happen to us; we are passively guided through it as if floating down a stream. I was like this, too, until I seriously put myself to task with my *magickal* work. I became more proactive and changed my personality so that I am happier. I moved to a new location, I consciously decided on a career, and I found my life partner. I used spells to help create my life rather than waiting for my life to happen to me. Most of the spells tend to be short and relatively easy, but some are longer, more complex, or repeated over time.

So what exactly is a spell? And what makes a spell work? A spell is a wish turned into ritual, a formal request made through spoken words or action or both. You decide you want something to change, and you focus energy specifically toward that goal. There are an infinite number of variations in creating spells from chanting catchy rhymes to lighting candles. Each variation will produce a slightly different result in either how you get what you want, when you get it, or what it is that actually comes to you. All the different parts of a spell, what you say, what you mix together, and what you burn or bury or submerge in water, all help focus your will.

A wish is different from a spell. Wishes and hopes are passing thoughts. They're important to note, but they don't usually make waves in the world at large because they're nothing more than transitory thoughts. A focused thought can become part of a spell, but a thought without that focus is much less likely to gain enough power to cause a change. Because spells use an accompanying ritual, for example, an incantation or gesticulation, your wish combines with your energy to give a deliberate, powerful force that makes changes.

A prayer is also different from a spell. A prayer is a petition to a spirit being to make a change in the world. Usually this is a divine power such as God (the Judeo-Christian God) or any of the many older gods or goddesses, for example Isis or Thor. But a prayer could also be a request to a saint, an angel, an undine (water sprite), or one of the many other beings that belongs to the ethereal world rather than to the physical earth. The person who is praying is not responsible for the change, just for his or her request. If what is prayed for happens, it is not due to the person who prayed but to the spirit that heard and answered the prayer. When you cast a spell, you are the one making the change. The web of energy starts with the spellcaster, and changes happen because of this person's energy. Not so with the prayer because it requires intervention. It is less powerful than a spell because the change comes secondhand if at all.

A simple "wish upon a star" is a form of a spell. And it works. Don't be misled if a spell seems to be too simple to be real. A simple spell has power. Actually, the simpler the spell, the more effective it often is. It can be hard to sustain focus for a long time. It is easier to cast a spell with a short burst of energy.

Magick is particularly good at making things happen when you know what you want but can't imagine how it could happen. For example, when I took American history, the teacher bored me to tears, and it seemed as if I were doomed to suffer. When I'd asked, I'd been told that all the other American history classes were completely full. After casting a spell to alleviate the situation, I suddenly found halfway through the year that a spot had opened up in the honors American history class, so I switched. If you were to do the same spell or even a different spell for the same goal, you wouldn't necessarily switch to another class. You might find a replacement teacher comes into your class after your teacher takes a leave of absence, or you might find a new way to connect with the teacher so that you no longer feel trapped. A spell goes into the world and gently tugs the web of energy that connects all people, animals, plants, and things. By effecting small changes in many other areas, the world opens up for the new reality you requested so that the change you desire will come about in the least disruptive way.

While each individual spell is one small ritual and can be cast by itself, together those in this book will give you considerable experience at wielding magick. You have immense power within yourself, which you can use to shape the life you want. As you progress through the sixty spells in this book, you'll discover the knowledge of how to cast the spells. Some of the spells won't relate to your life. Some are for specifically masculine or feminine spellcasters, and some spells relate to situations not relevant to your life. If you don't have acne, there's no need to cast a spell to get rid of it. Each spell also has a section afterward with an insight to the magickal world that will help you as you cast the spells in this book and ever after. Even if you don't cast all the spells, reading the magickal wisdom sections will help you considerably.

In chapter 1 you'll become a seeker. You'll learn how to *ground and center* and to cast the *circle*, and you'll cast nine spells to find your spellcasting tools. In chapter 2 you'll become a *dedicant*, someone who has pledged to explore magick. All nine spells relate to the body, and you'll learn about spells to create changes in your body. Chapter 3 has twelve spells, more than any other chapter. You'll become an apprentice and cast spells related to school and studying. For the eight spells in chapter 4, you'll become a sorcerer as you cast spells about your personal interests.

This includes your extracurricular time from sports to theater and from babysitting to art. Then in chapter 5, you'll have seven spells as a diviner that all relate to your home and family life. In chapter 6, you'll become a charmer and have eight spells relating to friends. And finally in chapter 7, you'll become an enchanter with seven spells about dating and love to help you get kisses, dates, relationships, and ultimately true love.

At the end of each chapter, you'll receive answers to the following key questions. I call these *adeptitudes*. After assimilating the knowledge of how to cast the spells and the points of magickal wisdom accompanying them, these adeptitudes reveal major insights for the long-term spellcaster:

What is your greatest psychic power?
What is the most powerful force behind spells?
What is your most important tool?
How can you make your spells gain in intensity?
What can you do to make your magick the most effective possible?
What is the greatest law of magick?
What is the key to living a magickal life?

The spells are collected into chapters by theme and organized so that they get progressively more difficult. If you do these spells and chapters in order, you will build your ability and become better at working magick. Everyone has the latent potential to cast spells and work magick, but few take the time or effort to develop it into a useful skill and put it into practice. But if you have to get to one in particular right away, it should be easy to find. You will, however, be more effective with the spell if you have built up to it by casting the ones before it. Also, I encourage you to take your time in casting these spells. Even if you read through the whole book quickly, leave at least a day and preferably longer between each spell you cast.

At the beginning of each chapter, I present a meditation to help you ground and center, followed by a way to cast the circle and call the *quarters*, the spirit forces at the compass points which guard and protect the circle. This prepares you for the spell and creates a sacred space in which to cast the spell. It's your portal *between the worlds* of the living and spirit. If you skip this part, your spell might work, but more likely, it'll fizzle and will not turn out the way you want. Your spells will be much more effective if you prepare yourself and your surroundings magickally. In the first chapter, you'll also learn how to take down this sacred space. This is called "devoking." You will use this same, simple method for every spell in the book. Probably you'll never find the word *devoke* in the dictionary, but it means to send away, which, you'll notice, is the opposite of invoke, to call in.

Each spell in this book has three parts. The first part is the list of what you'll need and what thoughts you'll need to consider before casting the spell. This process will help you get into the right frame of mind for the particular magickal work you're about to do in casting each spell. You'll see how to focus your thoughts, and you'll get information about the items you need during the spell so that you can collect them in a magickal way. Focusing your mind is extremely important when casting spells, and this is why the beginning sections help you get into the right frame of mind even before you start grounding and centering and then casting the circle in order to call the quarters.

The second part is the actual spell that you'll cast. Once you've entered sacred space, you'll work on the spell. Each spell has directions for what to do once you're in sacred space. Sometimes you'll find information about what not to think about. Most often you'll hear that you shouldn't think about the opposite of the result you want or specific people. In these cases, consciously turn your focus to something else about the spell.

The third part is that after each spell you'll find a point of magickal wisdom about the way that magick works. After you've cast your spell and it's working to manifest what you've directed, you may feel that the magickal wisdom is unnecessary. The points of magickal wisdom, however, give valuable information that will help you cast the spells effectively throughout this book and after you put it down when you're creating your own. You'll also see that every magickal wisdom is connected to every other like a jigsaw puzzle so that when you know them all, you'll have a much better idea of how the web of magickal energy works.

You've probably noticed that I've been spelling the word *magick* with a k on the end. It's a different word than the one you're accustomed to. "Magic" is amusing sleight of hand, tricks where the hand is faster than the eye. In

other words, magic without the *k* refers to illusions created to entertain. Magick with the *k* refers to changes
made in the world that aren't explainable through usual
means, are caused by people, and affect people, situations,
events, living creatures, or spirits. So you see, with magic
it looks like something has happened, but really nothing
has, and with magick something has happened, although
the cause may seem unexplainable. Magic already has a
meaning that's indelible in our collective consciousness,
which is why I prefer to have a slightly different spelling
as a reminder that change happens and magick is real.

Okay, let's go cast some spells.

CHAPTER 1

THE SEEKER: SPELLS ABOUT YOUR ROOM

YOU STAND AT THE GATEWAY ready to cross into the world of magick. Are you ready? Only you will know for sure, but you will never know what might happen if you don't try. In the chapter ahead of you, you'll begin by learning the process of preparing yourself for working magick, which we call grounding and centering. Then you'll learn how to cast a circle by calling the quarters to create sacred, protected space and later to dismantle it. These are skills you'll use for every spell you cast in this book. Don't gloss over them in order to move on to the spells. Your spells will be much more effective if you start properly each time. At first, it may take some time to do them, but soon you'll be able to do them quickly.

In the first spell, you'll sanctify your room as a sacred space. Next, you'll consecrate a notebook to use as your book of shadows. Then you'll set up your altar as a sort of home base for your spellcraft. You'll move on to *charging* an item of clothing for your magickal work. Charging means storing energy within an item for a specific purpose. From there you'll set out to find your tools one by one. In the last spell of the chapter you'll create a good luck talisman.

After you cast each spell, write about it in your book of shadows. Also, include each *magickal* experience that follows as a result of it. For example, when you cast the spell to find your wand, it won't materialize in your hand immediately. You'll probably find it sometime in the days following soon after casting the spell, and when you do, it's good to write about the experience in your book of shadows even though you may have written about casting the spell some time ago. Perhaps it'll seem that you're just gathering items before starting the spells in the next chapters. But if you take the time to focus, you'll realize that you're working magick just by doing these first spells. Sure, you could grab your favorite mug and use it as your cup. Why not if you already know that's your special cup and you want it for your altar? The answer is that going through the magickal process will help you develop your abilities, and you'll confirm that your mug is your spiritual tool. You give power to yourself, the cup, and your connection together by working in a magickal way.

As a seeker, you're marked by having many questions. Naturally, you'll have a skeptical mind. Why should I do this? Why not? If you start working with energy, which you'll need to do if you want to cast spells, you'll realize that the world is connected more intricately than you imagined, and you'll investigate how. As you turn the page, keep your mind open to all possibilities because if you've a set mind about what you'll find, then you'll miss the subtle tips that the magickal world sends your way. It's not bad to question yourself as well as the magickal process each step of the way because blind faith will lead you just as far astray as having no faith. Your magickal journey will be different from everyone else's as sometimes you'll meander and sometimes you'll jump straight ahead in leaps and bounds. Be gentle on yourself because you'll have to give yourself time with your own process between the worlds.

At the end of the chapter as a culmination of your time as a seeker, you'll learn an insight of *magickal mastery*. You'll discover the answer to the following question: What is your greatest psychic power?

Grounding and Centering

In the beginning you'll need to prepare yourself to do magickal work. You do this by meditating to *ground and center*. Grounding is making yourself firmly rooted on earth. It's the opposite of a lightheaded or floating feeling. Centering is feeling well balanced within yourself. The opposite is feeling pulled away or out of control of your own actions and thoughts. The point of grounding and centering before casting your spell is to put yourself in the most balanced place so that your spell is accurate and forceful. It's kind of like shooting an arrow. If you plant your feet apart so that you're in a steady position and if you draw the cord back far enough, you'll shoot the arrow and have a good chance of hitting the target. But if you stand with your feet together holding the bow in one hand and the arrow in the other, you can't expect your arrow to go anywhere near the target. The same is true of casting a spell. You have to prepare yourself first, and then you can cast a spell.

Here is your grounding and centering meditation for the spells in this chapter. Do this before each spell in this chapter. If you do the spells in order, you'll probably have practiced the meditation often enough so that you won't need to read it by the time you reach chapter 2. By breathing deeply and visualizing yourself as a tree, you'll ground and center. Don't try too hard to ground and center. Concentrate more on the breathing and visualizing yourself like a tree, and the grounding and centering will happen naturally.

Grounding and Centering Meditation: The Tree

Stand with your feet wide apart and stable.
Breathe deeply, exhale slowly.
Put your arms up straight into the air.
Breathe deeply, exhale slowly. Relax and let your shoulders sag down.
Let your arms widen so that they are 90 degrees apart (45 degrees between your head and each arm).
Picture your feet as roots growing down into the earth, your hands as branches reaching up to the sky, your torso as a tree trunk stretching to connect your

whole self. Imagine each blood vessel like a tree's
conduit for sap.

Breathe deeply, exhale slowly, and bring your arms
and hands down to your sides.

When you feel stable and grounded and firmly in the
center of your being as if you were a tree, continue
to cast the circle.

Casting the Circle

Now that you've prepared yourself by grounding and centering, you'll need to create a sacred space in which to cast
your spells. This is the process of defining the circle and
calling quarters, the guardians from the four directions. A
circle is a protective space, impermeable by outside forces
without your explicit invitation to join you in the circle.
Spirits from each of the four compass points will watch
over the space when you ask them to do so. These
guardian spirits are called East, South, West, and North,
and reside in their directions. They are respectively allied
with the spirits Air, Fire, Water, and Earth. Center is also
a spirit force. When you have set up this sacred space,
you'll be ready to set your magick in motion.

Here is how to cast the circle and call the quarters for
the spells in this chapter. It's a basic, simple method that
features the natural elements which correspond to each of
the compass directions. It's easy to learn and has the
advantage that it'll work well no matter where you are.

Circle Casting: The Elements

Starting in the north, walk around your circle three times imagining a ring of light that is left behind you as you walk. Each time you pass north, envision the ring of light becoming stronger and more vibrant. After the third time, come to a stop and stand in the north for a moment. Feel the ring of energy you have just created.

From where you are standing quietly in the north, turn and face east, extend your arms with your hands facing palms out and call to the quarters.

In the east, say, "I call to East and welcome Air." Visualize air blowing. Feel it whooshing past your body.

Turn to the south, and say, "I call to South and welcome Fire." Visualize fire burning. Feel the heat of a fire on your body.

Turn to the west, and say, "I call to West and welcome Water." Visualize water flowing. Feel water splashing on your body.

Turn to the north, and say, "I call to North and welcome Earth." Visualize trees planted in the ground. Feel the pull on your feet as you walk through mud.

Your circle is cast, and the quarters are called. You are between the worlds. Here you are ready to do magick.

Devoking

Did you think you were ready to jump into a spell? Well, in one way you are. But I also have to tell you how to take down the sacred circle you've created to cast your spell. This process is called "devoking." You create this circle to protect you each time you do your work. But after you're done, you'll need to go back to your regular life. You can set up a circle to stay and reinforce it by casting it again each time you work there. For example, if you've a separate room you intend to use only as a temple, but much more often you'll want to be able to take down your magickal space. It gives you the freedom to create sacred space wherever you go.

Usually, you'll want to give a lot of thought to where you're going to set up a continuing circle. Your room could be this place, but it's also possible that it's not. Before you choose a long-term spot, give yourself some time. If you know how to set up and take down a circle, you'll have flexibility no matter where you are when you want to do this. This empowers you greatly. You don't have to go to a specific spot to practice magick, and you don't have to depend on anyone else to do it for you.

Devoking: Ending Thanks

Start in the north, and say, "Thank you guardians of the North and Earth. Farewell."
Turn to the west, and say, "Thank you guardians of the West and Water. Farewell."

Turn to the south, and say, "Thank you guardians of
the South and Fire. Farewell."

Turn to the east, and say, "Thank you guardians of the
East and Air. Farewell."

Walk around your circle counterclockwise again from
north through west and south and east to north where you
began. As you do so, visualize the bright light of the circle
dimming and dissipating.

At the end of this process, stand in the center and make
a thumping noise by clapping or stomping a foot. Do it
once in a definitive manner or three times to make it cer-
tain. If it's a loud noise, it settles the energy at once, but if
there's a need for quiet, you can make a soft, tapping noise
and be just as effective. As you do this, visualize the
excess energy of the spell and circle draining down in a
big whoosh into the ground. Try it different ways, and see
what feels most appropriate to you, keeping in mind that
you may feel the need for a slightly different way each
time. At various times after the spells, I'll make a specific
suggestion that has worked particularly well for me, but
see what works for you.

Notice that when you cast the circle, you do so in a
clockwise motion that winds up energy. But when you
devoke, do so in a counterclockwise motion that unwinds
the energy.

From now on throughout the book, you'll use this same
process of devoking to bring down the circle.

Getting Rid of Waste After Spells Are Cast

After casting some spells, you'll have unwanted scraps left over when you're done. When you burn candles, they drip and wax creates a puddle. When you cut paper or string, you may have excess scraps. When you eat or drink during a spell, you may have food or beverage left over. I'm not talking about an item, such as a talisman or charm, that you made during the spell; I'm talking about what's not used to make that item. You can't just dump these items in the trash. You've charged them with your energy and intention during the spell, and you must release that energy before disposing of the debris.

You can easily release the charge of energy and intention after spells in a couple of ways. One way is to sprinkle salt over the debris. Another is to bury it. Another is to freeze it. Another is to throw it into water (down a drain or in a stream or pond). When choosing how you'll dispose of excess material, consider if it's biodegradable or not. If it's not, then burying it or throwing it into the water isn't a great option. It's fine, however, to pour beverages onto the ground outside or to bury food. The most important aspect of whatever method you choose is to be intentional about it. You can even get rid of waste from spells by putting it in the trash as long as you're doing so as a conscious rather than perfunctory act. Be mindful of returning these items to the earth from which they came. Be thankful for being able to use the parts you needed for your spell. Visualize the excess energy returning to the earth as you throw the material away.

The Spells

Spell 1: For Keeping One's Room Private

YOU WILL NEED:

> water
> salt
> candle
> matches

You will also need to know where east, south, west, and north are in your room. If you don't have a compass, which is the easiest way to figure out where north is, then take a day to watch the path of the sun. It rises in the east; so if you watch where it comes up, you'll know where east is. It sets in the west; so if you see the sun as it sets, you'll know where west is.

As you prepare for this spell, think of your room as your sanctuary. It's a place you can retreat to to be alone and feel safe when you need to, a sort of home base. You should feel free to express yourself there and have your room reflect you. With this protection in place, you'll be able to work magick in your room. You can protect it magickally even if other people need to go into it from time to time. This ritualized spell will seal your room for you. It'll become a sacred space for you.

As you gather materials, think about how salt water is like water in a womb that nurtures and supports the life it surrounds.

The Spell: Ground and center. Cast the circle.

Once you are in sacred space, light the candle. Stand in the center of the circle and hold the container of water. Think about the cleansing you are about to do in order to prepare your room for a new purpose.

Take the salt and sprinkle it on the water. Mix it up a little bit. Hold the cup of salty water in both your hands. Cup your hands around the cup as if your hands would themselves cup the water if you didn't have the container there.

Walk to the north holding the salty water close to your chest with both hands. Stand there silently and extend the cup out in front of you, almost as if you were giving it to the north. Hold it there for a moment, and bring it back to your chest. Walk to the east and stand there. Now put your fingers into the salty water, and sprinkle droplets of water by flicking them off your fingers. Do this in each direction of your room starting at the east and moving around the compass points to the south, to the west, and to the north. Your room should not look like it was flooded. If you do this correctly, nobody will even see water around the room, even though you interrupt your spell (which we know won't happen because you chose a time when you're unlikely to be bothered in the first place).

When you have finished that, put the water down and stand in the center of the room again. Hold your arms up slightly above shoulder height and extended out to the side with your palms facing up.

In a strong voice say:

> By East, by South, by West, by North,
> Powers of the divine come forth.
> This is my room, my special place,
> May the divine protect my sacred space.

Stand there with your arms out and wait for a moment. Then crouch down on your feet as close to fetal position as you can get. Stay there a moment quietly. Now stand up straight and say: "So mote it be."

Devoke.

Your spell is cast. Once again, your room will not look any different to you or anyone else who goes into it. But it'll henceforth be your protected place. It'll feel different to anyone sensitive to psychic energies. This doesn't mean that people won't go into it. It would be too difficult for you to explain why you didn't want friends or family members to go into your room while you're living in a house with other people. Parents and siblings probably assume they have the right to enter pretty much whenever they want to regardless of your magick. But people who do go in will have more trouble finding what they're looking for. They won't see obvious things. They'll tend to forget why they went in. The magick will divert their attention.

I suggest that you sit down at some point after doing the spell, but before sleeping, to write a brief recap of what you did, how it felt, and any thoughts you have about it. Writing will help you to process the experience.

Magickal Wisdom: Casting a circle creates a sacred, protected space.

The work you did created a safe, sacred space temporarily. This is called a "circle," and it can be used whenever you want to be in a protected place. There are other more elaborate ways to embellish this, but this is the basic format. A circle has no corners. And because the rim of a circle is the same all the way around, there's no break where it can come apart. Do not cross the borders of your circle while it's up. Treat it as a magickal wall that you can't walk through just as you can't walk through a physical wall. (If for some reason you need to leave during a circle, you can *cut out* by erecting a magickal door to go through. Visualize a door as a frame of light. It often helps to direct the energy from your hand or finger to delineate where the energy is. After coming back in, remember to seal the circle closed by visualizing the light dissipating from that doorframe or by making a brushing gesture with your hands where you'd previously put the door.) Repeating this spell a few times, especially at regular intervals, will magickally reinforce your room as your sanctuary.

Spell 2: For Consecrating Your Book of Shadows

YOU WILL NEED:
    notebook (preferably one with a spiral binding)
    art supplies to decorate it (for example, acrylic paints,
        colored pens or pencils, or glue and collage
        materials such as magazine clippings or photos)

The first step in preparing for this spell is to find a notebook that you'll use for the sole purpose of writing about the spells you cast. Many people buy journals with fancy leather bindings or expensive handmade papers. While these are beautiful, people tend to avoid writing in them unless they think their thoughts and handwriting will be perfect. Your book of shadows should be a place in which you can make mistakes freely. You need to be able to change your mind, cross out a word in favor of another, and write arrows pointing to other areas. No teacher is going to read it, so you don't need to worry about spelling, grammar, or handwriting. It's yours, and only you need know what it says and what it means later on. I suggest an ordinary spiral notebook because a book of shadows is a tool associated with Center. The spiral is a symbol associated with the dominion of balance, transformation, and the journey, especially as depicted in the maze or labyrinth. So the spiral binding signifies this type of notebook as a tool associated with balance and the center of the sacred circle.

Concentrate on your magickal journal and on how it'll become an extension of you. The journal becomes a physical manifestation of the internal process you'll undergo by casting spells. In this way it will be like a supersecret diary. Not only will it include your personal thoughts and emotions, but also it will include details about spirituality, which can be intensely intimate. Not everyone believes in the spirit world because it's not visible. And some people believe that casting spells is wrong. So, there's more at stake than a normal diary getting into the wrong hands.

More than anything, a journal allows you to face yourself. If you lie in your journal, it hurts nobody but you. Because it is a place to be honest with yourself, it can be tremendously balancing for you. Your book of shadows not only will contain information about spells you cast and your insights about magick, but it will help you find your core purpose in life.

Consecration is a way of making a spiritual dedication. You will go into sacred space and state your purpose for the tool. By doing so, you will charge it with the intention to be different from an ordinary notebook. You will turn it into your book of shadows.

The Spell: Stand tall in the center of your room. Breathe deeply and regularly while you go through the grounding and centering meditation. Then cast the circle.

Sit down on the floor and hold your notebook. Rub the front cover in clockwise circles with both your hands so that the entire palm of your hand is touching it. Feel how your energy makes it warm. Then turn it over and do the same to the back cover.

Take out your art supplies, and decorate the front cover. Use colors that match your identity, that reflect you in some way. The design doesn't have to be meaningful to anyone else; only you have to be able to understand it. Put symbols on the cover that signify what's really important to you to make it yours. To me owls are special. They're nocturnal and wise, and I've worked on my ability to see in the dark, both by walking around outside at night and also by developing spiritually. So I put an owl on mine. I also suggest that you put a symbol of Center on it. I put a spiral in the middle of the owl's stomach because the spiral, nautilus, and labyrinth all represent the journey to the center of the self. But you could also put a picture of an apple core on yours, and that would be just as symbolic of Center (get it, core/center?).

Then stand up facing east, and hold the notebook against your forehead, and say, "May this book of shadows be a safe place to express my thoughts."

Then face south, and hold the notebook against your stomach, and say, "May this book of shadows be a safe place to express my gut intuition."

Then face west, and hold the notebook against your chest to your heart, and say, "May this book of shadows be a safe place to express my feelings."

Then face north, and hold the notebook behind you against your back, and say, "May this book of shadows be a safe place to express what happens to me."

Next, you need to make a commitment to use it. You need to state your intention to fill this book of shadows with your writing about spells. You shouldn't make a promise that you're not going to keep, so think carefully about what you can say. Don't say that you'll write ten pages every day unless you know you can do it. Set yourself up to keep the vow you'll make. I started by saying, "I will write in this book of shadows after each spell I cast."

Devoke.

Write in your book of shadows after each spell. I also suggest that you start by writing what you can remember about the spell that you cast to protect your room, and then write about this consecration spell. Write the date, what you did, how you felt, and anything that seems noteworthy or especially interesting to you. It can be quick and easy. Don't think you have to write five pages about each spell. Maybe a paragraph will be enough. It's better to write something short about what you did than nothing at all.

Magickal Wisdom: A book of shadows is a magickal tool.

Keep a book of shadows of your personal magickal journey. Magick is unseen, and writing down your experiences gives them validity. Memory is not so kind in the magickal world. Later after the spells, either you'll remember something as really significant when in fact you had to work hard to realize, hey, yeah that really was magick, or you may forget the details of a spell or even that you cast the spell at all. Writing a book of shadows helps you recognize them as "real." It also gives you a record of what you did when so that you can make your own discoveries about magick. It should include both the knowledge you've acquired of how to cast spells and also the wisdom you've gained through the process of using that knowledge. Many people give up keeping their magickal journals, and yet it's one of the most important tools for anyone on a spiritual path because it shows personal growth so clearly. It takes time and commitment to keep it up, but I have never heard of anyone who regretted doing it. And I've yet to meet anyone who gave it up and didn't regret it later.

Spell 3: For Setting Up Your Altar

YOU WILL NEED:

your tools

new and small candle that will burn down during
   or shortly after the spell

damp cloth

incense

matches

Sit quietly in your sacred space. Look around you and think about what an altar is. An altar is a place to sit quietly and reflect on our lives, to discover who we are, or to just find stillness. We can all benefit from a place to put special items that have significance to us. Most families have a tabletop with photos of the people they love—and, whether they'd agree or not, this is a kind of altar. An altar can be as informal or elaborate as you make it.

An altar can have several functions. It's a place where you will keep your magickal tools, including your book of shadows and the tools in the upcoming spells in this chapter. You'll only put sacred items there, and items that aren't sacred don't belong there. Thus, it'll become a surface that'll signal that the items there are special in this way. An altar is also a place where you'll work magick, and in this way it's a tool associated with North and its qualities including stability, security, and physical manifestation. On the practical side, you'll need your altar to be a flat surface so that you can use it while casting spells. During your rituals, you'll often need to burn candles and incense. Your altar must be a safe place where you can have fire. You may need to put hot liquids there such as tea. You may also need to put snow or ice there, so it shouldn't be a surface that can get damaged if wet. But perhaps most important of all, it must be a place that feels comfortable to you. If your altar is functioning in your magickal life, you'll be able to go there whenever you want to meditate, clarify your feelings, and cast spells. If it doesn't feel comfortable to you, then you won't go there, and the purpose of having an altar will be defeated.

Think about how you will sit or stand in front of your altar. Some people like to have the altar near a window to look outside. Others would find this distracting. Many people like to sit in a chair in front of an altar, while others prefer a cushion on the floor. What height is right for your altar? Is there a particular piece of furniture that is special to you and ideal for this purpose? The top of a dresser, a desktop, or a shelf might be perfect. Your bed is not a wise choice because mattresses are squishy, and your tools might fall over when you sit down. Think about where you would be situated in the room if you were sitting in front of your altar. Would your back be to the door making it hard to hear or see potential interruptions before they happen? Maybe it would be preferable not to do that. It is up to you.

Keep in mind that you may have the perfect surface for the altar, but you may need to rearrange your furniture in order for it to feel like it's in the right place. This may not be ideal because someone else may ask you why you rearranged your furniture, and you'll have to give an answer. Depending on who it is, saying "It's so I could put my new altar over there" may open a can of worms that you don't want to deal with, so think about what you'll say beforehand. While it's traditional to have an altar in the north, it's more important to have it in a place that feels calm and welcoming to you where you're going to feel strong casting spells.

It's fine to have a special outdoor place for this as well. An outside sacred space can be great for meditating or casting spells or simply feeling a deep connection to the natural world. It's probably not a great place, however, to keep magickal items. They can be damaged or lost due to rain, snow, wind, sunlight, or people passing by. So I suggest that you find an indoor place for your altar, and if you want a special place under the sun or moon, that's fine too, but not for the same purpose as the indoor altar.

You're ready to begin once you've identified which surface will become your altar and rearranged your room, if necessary. You should also be able to articulate why you want this altar and how you plan to use it. An altar is a symbol of your decision to explore magick and to cultivate your psychic abilities. Your altar will be a place to keep your tools, to cast your spells, and to find the stillness within yourself that you'll need to connect with your subconscious. It's fine to start with just one or two items on it and expand slowly. It's a space for what you need from it magickally; it doesn't matter if you only burn candles and never burn incense—it's your intention to pay attention to inner messages that matters. You don't have to promise to give up your firstborn baby in exchange for power, but you do need to be aware that your life will change in ways you can't know or expect if you follow this path. Your current plan is good enough reason to set up an altar for now. Over time, the way you use your altar may change, and that's fine too.

I also want to add a note about short-lasting candles. These aren't so easy to find because most candles are made to be long-lasting, so that they're a good value for their cost. I've found that menorah candles for Chanukah tend to last only an hour. That's a good length for most spells. Also, they often come in different, pretty colors and designs.

The Spell: Stand in front of your altar to be. Prepare yourself by grounding and centering. Cast the circle.

Take a deep breath and let it out.

Take a damp cloth, and wipe off your altar to clean it. Use a counterclockwise, circular motion, which intrinsically banishes bad energy and previous intentions as well as dust.

Now light some incense. My favorite is a stick of sage because of its strong purifying quality, but you can use another scent if you don't have sage or if you have another strong preference. Waft the smoke over the entire altar's surface. By doing this, you're preparing this surface for its new purpose. You're also infusing this surface with your energy.

State your purpose: "I have cleaned this surface. It was ordinary, but from this time forward, it will be my altar. It is a special place where I can come to work magick. Henceforth it is sacred."

Now place the candle that you brought for this purpose in the center of the altar and light it. This is to honor your new altar. It's an offering you're making to it to celebrate the spirit of this sacred place. As the candle burns, state your intention to put your tools, including your athame, wand, and cup, when you have them, on the altar.

Let the candle burn down until it's finished. After the candle has burned down, say, "So mote it be," and blow a kiss into the air to seal your work.

Devoke.

Magickal Wisdom: Everyone recognizes magick uniquely. Magick doesn't need be recognizable as magick to anyone else but you. Someone who practices magick may recognize a magickal item or act, but a person who isn't attuned to magick probably wouldn't. Even another person who practices magick may not know which items are your magickal tools. That doesn't mean that there's less magick in them. It means that you can perceive it better in these tools than that other person can. Just as snowflakes and fingerprints are unique, every person has a different energy, as does every animal, plant, or object. In fact, anytime you interact with someone or something else, you're coming into contact with a different energy. Different combinations are more obvious and feel better to some people and are less obvious and feel worse to others.

Anytime you have an immediate gut reaction, positive or negative, you're perceiving how the new energy interacts with yours.

Spell 4: For Hallowing a Garment

YOU WILL NEED:

    quiet place where you can be alone

    candle

    matches

    vanilla extract

    your garment

When you put on clothes, your mindset changes. When you dress up in your sports clothes, you're mentally preparing to play. When you choose clothes to go out on a date, you're focusing on being with that person and deciding what you're going to do. When you're getting dressed for school, you're thinking about all your friends, teachers, and everyone else who is going to see you and about what you'll be comfortable wearing all day. When you were a young kid, you put on a costume at Halloween to go ask for candy and, perhaps, make a little mischief. The costume put you in the mood for it. Perhaps you didn't notice it consciously, but when you think about it, you can see how the clothes make a subtle difference. When you cast spells, it also helps to wear a special garment to get ready for doing magick. You don't have to wear it when you're casting every spell in this book, but if it's convenient, it'll help you focus and raise energy more quickly. And the more you focus and raise energy, the more effective your magick will be.

First, you have to choose which item of clothing it'll be. As you're looking through your drawers and closet, pull out a few possible garments and throw them on your bed. When you have them all on your bed, think to yourself about each one. I suggest you pick something that is basic and comfortable and that you can wear no matter what you're doing. Underwear can be a good choice because usually nobody else sees it. But you can't wear underwear more than one day a week unless you like to wash your clothes, and it requires that you take off your pants and change into the underwear before casting a spell and out of it again after a spell.

A shirt or jacket is another great choice. Personally, I love my blue jeans. A hooded sweatshirt can also be a good selection because there's something to the feeling of pulling a hood over your head that helps you feel different from when the hood is down. Are there any that you veto because you can't wear them when you want to cast spells? For example, mittens won't work so well in summer. You should also be able to keep the item of clothing you're going to wear for spellcraft for a long time. Don't choose the sweater you "borrowed" from your sister because she might want to put it back in her dresser when she finds it. Narrow your top choices down to two or three.

Touch each of the two or three choices. Feel the energy in each one? Try not to think too hard or you'll impose a response. Just close your eyes and try to find stillness within yourself. If you're quiet within yourself, you'll be ready if it says anything to you. Remember the special things about it. Did your older brother give it to you? Did you buy it at your favorite store? Did you have your first kiss while wearing it? Did you win the bowling league championship while in it? Keep all of that in mind.

Choose one. No, not two for different occasions. You can do this later to another item if you really want to, but you need to concentrate on just one item at a time so that you can get that magick in it. One will come to the front as the obvious choice for this particular working. Trust your intuition. Keep it out and put the others away. Again, this helps keep the focus on this one item of clothing so that it will absorb the power you put into it.

The Spell: Ground and center. Cast the circle.

Light your candle, and pick up your garment. Take a moment to feel it in your hands and to reflect on it.

There is no rush, so take your time. When you are ready, say in a strong but not necessarily loud voice, "The reason my garment is special is (and here you give your individual reason that it's special)." You can add to that. If this is your special item, you probably have more than one reason. So in the same firm tone of voice continue talking about your special clothes. For your last sentence about why the clothing is special, say something about how you feel when you wear it. It should be some sort of good, positive feeling. For example, this is what I said about my jeans: "When I wear these jeans I feel I can truly be me and that these jeans help me follow my own personal path." And now for your final statement, use your strong, firm, sure-of-yourself voice, and say, "From now on when I wear this garment, I will work magick for the greater good of all."

Then take out the vanilla extract and put a drop on your finger. Dab drops at intervals on the edges, seams, and hems. When choosing where to put the vanilla, think about putting it on the fabric's seams and the parts that rest on important parts of your body as you wear it (for a shirt, this might be the neck, wrists, and belly button, and for pants, the waist, ankles, and crotch). Now hold your item up over your head for thirty to sixty seconds.

Then bring it down and place it on the ground (not next to your candle—you don't need your garment to catch fire). Say, "So mote it be" in that same, firm voice. Now blow out your candle.

Devoke and end by clapping your hands together three times with sharp, staccato beats.

You have cast your spell. Your clothing has changed. It may not be noticeable now, but later on something subtle will probably happen that will show you that it happened. Your garment won't look any different from the clothes you regularly wear. It's the kind of clothing that will fool people looking at it because they will have no idea that you're wearing a consecrated, magickal item.

Magickal Wisdom: Restrict magickal items for magickal use.

Wearing your magickal clothing when you cast spells or work other magick will imbue the clothing with more magick. The repeated wearing acts as a sort of reinforcement in which you recharge it. For the same reason, wearing your garment throughout the day when you're not doing magick will dissipate the magickal energy you charged your garment with, so don't wear it unless it's for the purpose of doing magick. There may be times when you have to wear the garment for a while before and after the spell in order to be wearing it during the spell (for example, if you're going to cast a spell while at school), and that's fine. You may want to do this spell again after the time that you had to wear it outside the circle to recharge it. Therefore, choose your garment carefully so that this won't be a problem (for example, a hat is portable, and you could whip it out just for the spell). Go ahead and wear your special shirt, pants, or sweatshirt when you next decide to cast a spell and see how wearing it helps you go between the worlds.

Spell 5: For Calling Your Athame to You

YOU WILL NEED:

stone or piece of metal that you are willing to part with (for example, a small pebble or an abandoned nail)

yellow candle

matches

trowel (small shovel)

No matter what you do in life, it's easier if you have the right tools. An athame (pronounced: uh-THAH-may) is a knife used for pointing and directing energy outward in a ritual, but it's never used to cut anything physically. It works as an extension of your arm, hand, and finger to project energy forward. Traditionally, it's a black-handled, double-edged knife or a sword, but it's more important that the tool feels right to you for your work than whether it has a double edge or a black handle. Even if you already have an athame, cast this spell and go through the process again. Either you'll have confirmation that your athame is right for you or you might find out that it's time for a new tool. This spell will help you find the right athame for your magickal work.

The athame is an important tool, and you should have one to work magick, which is why it's the first tool you'll set out to find. It doesn't have to have a sharp blade because you'll never use it to cut anything. You'll use it to direct energy, so it should feel comfortable in your hand and powerful to use. You'll have it for a long time, conceivably for the rest of your life. Also, it's a highly personal tool, so it's wise to choose carefully. This spell will help you find the right one for you.

Whenever you have needed a knife, you've gone to the kitchen and pulled one out of the drawer. It's an easy way to get a tool you need. Now, however, you need a knife to use as a spiritual tool. Like your spellcasting garment, it should only be used for magickal purposes. How do you know which knife will enhance your magick? Athames aren't exactly labeled on shelves in most stores!

There's a process to finding one. You're not going to go out and get it; you're going to ask it to come to you. Knives, of course, don't have legs and can't move on their own. But you're going to ask for a suitable knife to "find" you, to come across your path somehow. And you're going to open yourself to finding that knife because you have to recognize it when you see it.

As you prepare to do this spell, think of the different forms your athame could take. Try to be as inclusive as possible. Usually an athame is made of some sort of metal or mineral, but they come in all shapes and sizes. It could be a butter knife, a letter opener (often these are pretty as well as effective), a pair of scissors, or a quartz crystal with a point on the end even if it has a wooden or plastic handle.

The Spell: Ground and center. Cast your circle.

When you're between the worlds, stand in the center facing your altar and take another deep breath. Say, "I am between the worlds to call my athame to me." Light your yellow candle with this purpose in mind. Yellow corresponds to East, so this candle reinforces the energy you're putting out to find your athame which is a tool associated with East.

Take out your piece of stone or metal and hold it in your dominant hand (the one you write with). Concentrate on the many different forms an athame can take. Envision different types of metal and different types of minerals or stones. Since an athame is a tool associated with East, say, "Tool of knowledge, learning, and inspiration, find your way to me," as these qualities also correspond to East.

Hold the stone or metal in your hand close to your heart. As the stone or metal warms up in your hand, say, "Sword, Knife, Blade, see inside my head and heart and come to join my magickal purpose." Here you are talking to the spirit of the object that you're calling to you.

Standing in place while holding your stone or metal, spin around three times fast in a clockwise direction. Now go to the east in your circle, and say, "As I give back this stone (or metal), I call to my athame to find its way to me." Go back to the center of your circle and put the stone or metal down.

Then close the circle by devoking and clapping three times.

Your circle is now open so that you're no longer in magickal space, but you're not done. You have to give this stone or piece of metal back to the earth as an exchange for the athame you'll receive. Your athame usually won't come to you until after you've given up your gift. So, go outside with your trowel, and bury the stone or metal. It doesn't have to be deep in the earth, a few inches are fine. You can put it in your backyard, in a park, in a planted area with trees or shrubbery; even a houseplant will do in a pinch. You must not dig it up though. Soon your athame will come to you.

Magickal Wisdom: Everything has a spirit.

People have spirits, animals have spirits, plants have spirits, and, yes, things, including rocks and metal, have spirits too. All over the world every culture has at least some belief in people's spirits. Animals can move in ways similar enough to people, so that it's relatively easy to acknowledge the spirit in them. And plants, although they grow slowly, are alive and grow, so it's not a huge jump to understand that, yes, plants have spirits too. But it's tough for many people to accept that objects have a spirit because they're inanimate. All things come from natural resources, or they were produced with parts that are made from the earth. They're made of atoms, which have energy holding them together. An inanimate object may not be able to move or grow the way people, animals, and plants can, but it does have a spirit.

You can communicate with an object, and it'll respond, albeit in a subtle manner. By doing this spell, you're acknowledging that a knife has a spirit of its own, and that if it's a good knife for you, it'll want to share its purpose with yours. If you treat an object with respect, in a way that shows you know it has a spirit, you'll find it easy to use the object. For example, if you have a door with a lock that is usually sticky, after you show appreciation for the spirits of the key and lock, the lock may be a lot easier to open. This may seem silly at first, but try thinking in a way that acknowledges the spirit of things while casting this spell before you dismiss the idea as preposterous.

Spell 6: For Finding Your Wand

YOU WILL NEED:
   piece of wood that you are willing to part with
   red candle
   matches

You've no doubt seen wands in the hands of wizards in fantasy movies and magicians at magic shows. They point the wand, and a lightning bolt comes forth or a rabbit jumps out of a hat. Now I'm going to change all the rules. A wand isn't used for pointing and having energy go out from it. A wand is used to call energy to you. It's a receiver, not a giver like an athame. Unlike a knife that culminates in a point, many wands do not have one pointed end but two or more dull, flat ends. I've found that the entire stick of a wand is effective at receiving energy and funneling it to the person holding it. Magick is done by directing energy, not always pushing it out; thus at various times, you'll need to pull energy to you.

Think of the times that you've picked up pieces of wood. Probably at some point you picked up a wooden bat to play baseball or softball either for fun or on a team. Maybe you've handed a wooden cane to someone. And you've surely picked up a pencil. Perhaps at some point you pretended to be a magician, and you waved a magic wand in the air. All these pieces of wood could be used as wands. And now that you're intending to work magick, it's time to have a real wand.

Think of a divining rod. It's a piece of wood used to locate water. It typically has the shape of a letter Y, and the person who uses it is said to feel vibrations when holding the stick over underground water. A wand acts as your own personal divining rod, not so much to find water, but to feel the energy you receive when you call it to you. You can move great amounts of energy without depleting your own when you call energy to yourself with a wand, so with this process you can have spells much more powerful than if you used only your own energy without feeling exhausted afterwards. As you gather your materials together, keep this aspect of using a wand in mind.

It is not a steadfast rule that all wands are made of wood, but for the most part they are. Wood is good at receiving energy and spreading the energy so that it is not directed in one point like an athame but equalized over the entire body of the wand and over to you. I suggest that you concentrate on finding a wood one, at least in the beginning. Some examples of wands are a twig, a wooden rod, a pencil, a paintbrush, and a cane or a staff, which can be unwieldy at first, although some people swear by them.

The Spell: Ground and center. Cast your circle.

When you're finished, stand in the center. Take a deep breath. Light your red candle, and say, "I cast this circle and am between the worlds to locate my wand."

Hold your piece of wood in your nondominant hand. Walk to the south in your circle. Wands are tools equated with South and element Fire, so think about the burning drive to do anything you care about a lot and the hot summer sun and imagine holding your wand. Imagine how it will feel to receive energy. Say, "Somewhere in this world, a piece of wood has the potential to be my wand. I call to you stick, that you may realize your full potential as a wand in my hands."

Hold that small piece of wood in your nondominant hand, which naturally tends to be more receptive and less active, and make it into a fist. Put your fist on your stomach just above your belly button. Wands are associated with gut feelings, your intuition telling you something. A wand is a tool associated with South, so say, "Tool of passion, drive, and will, find your way to me."

Keeping your fist tightly around your piece of wood, crouch down into a tiny ball. Pull your energy in. Say, "As I release this piece of wood, my wand journeys to me and I open myself to receive it." Then in a sudden burst, jump up into the air.

Remain standing. Put down the piece of wood. Close your circle by devoking and clapping your hands. You have one last bit of work to do. Go outside during the day (if you've done this ritual at night, then wait until the next day), and put the small piece of wood in a tree, preferably stuck under a piece of bark sticking out or in the crook of branches.

Magickal Wisdom: Trust your intuition.

Your intuition will guide you in all matters magickal. As you look for your wand, try to let any little intuitive feeling come forward. Pay attention to it. Value it. Let it guide you. It's so easy to overlook or suppress your intuition, but really it's a major tool that will help you throughout life. As you deal with people, you use your intuition constantly. The more you listen to your intuition and follow it, the better you'll be at working magick and in finding your spiritual path in life. And you'll definitely end up with the perfect wand.

Spell 7: For Encountering Your Cup

YOU WILL NEED:
    4 disposable cups
    4 ordinary cups
    4 drinkable liquids
    candle
    matches

During your magickal work, you'll also need a cup, a tool associated with West that represents the power of dreams, wisdom, and emotions. Perhaps you have a special mug. Or perhaps you're more the type for an elegant goblet or a down-to-earth beer stein. You could also use an ordinary glass. You'll notice that while I have spells for identifying an athame and wand, I'm counting on you to know about cups in general because you have more experience with them. Most of us have a favorite cup already. Now it's time to find it, and ask it if it's appropriate for your magickal use.

As you gather the materials you need for this spell, keep in mind the basic purpose of cups. Cups can hold many things, but they are ideal for holding liquids. A container with holes in it cannot effectively hold liquid. Cups are often also used for drinking. Most cups don't have spouts and are only used in a pinch for pouring.

Get four disposable cups. Personally, I prefer paper

cups because they're more natural, but if you have to have plastic, that's okay too. Bring these to your sacred space.

Now you must choose four different beverages. One should probably be water because it is the basic, life-supporting fluid. It's fine if it's tap water or bottled, flat or carbonated. It's up to you how you like your water. You might also choose your favorite juice. For me, that's orange juice, but choose your favorite from apple juice to pomegranate. You might choose a tea as well. How about an herbal tea, a black or green tea, or traditional English Breakfast? You might choose a warm beverage such as warm cider or hot chocolate. Deliberate carefully about which four to use. You should like all of them. Maybe you love eggnog, cola, or milk. Pour a small amount of each of your four beverages into ordinary cups and bring them to your working space. (Note that your four disposable cups are still empty.) You will need to pour these beverages during the spell, so I recommend that you bring them to circle in containers with pouring spouts such as measuring cups that are used for baking.

Do not use alcoholic beverages unless you are over twenty-one and can drink them legally. Breaking the law is wrong. Stealing is also wrong, and stealing alcohol (for example, from a store or from your parents) will have a negative impact on your magick.

Finally, choose a candle to burn during this spell.

The Spell: When you've collected everything you'll need in the circle, stand quietly in your magickal space. Ground and center. Cast the circle.

Light your candle while thinking of the purpose of your spell.

Sit in the center of the circle facing whichever quarter best reflects your mood and personality. Light your candle. Breathe deeply and think clearly about cups and liquid and about how they are perfect for each other. Visualize the many shapes of cups, glasses, mugs, steins, and goblets. Slowly pour from the ordinary cups into the disposable cups each of the four liquids you chose. Then choose one and put it in the east; put another in the south; put a third in the west; and put the fourth in the north.

Go back to the center and breathe deeply once again. Say aloud, "As I drink (name the beverage you put in the east), my magickal cup comes closer to me." Then drink the beverage while you sit in the center. Be mindful of the way you drink that beverage. Do you take big gulps? Do you sip it little by little? Do you drink it quickly? Slowly? What type of cup do you usually use to drink this beverage you like so much? Let your mind be open to seeing the best type of cup for this drink. It may be your magickal cup. Drink until the disposable cup is empty. Repeat this process with each of the cups in clockwise order, going next to south, west, and then north.

When you are done, bring all the disposable cups into the center. Stack the empty cups together. As you are doing so, say, "I drank from these temporary cups so that I may find the cup for my magickal work. My magickal cup will hold (name each of the four beverages you just drank). I am open to finding the cup that is perfect for assisting me in my magickal work."

When you are done, take a deep breath, and say, "So mote it be." Blow out your candle. Nod your head to North, West, South, and East to devoke. Then clap your hands three times.

Over the next week, be on the lookout for your cup. It'll surface. You may know immediately as you do this spell which cup it'll be, but you may not. If you don't, then it may completely surprise you. You may know it as soon as you see it. You may have a sudden inspiration about where you're going to get it. It'll feel right. When you think you've found it, quietly ask it two questions: "Are you my cup?" and "Will you come with me to aid me in my magickal work?" Trust your intuition for the response.

Magickal Wisdom: An ordinary object can be magickal.

You've seen many cups in your life, and you've probably never thought, "Wow, that looks like a magickal vessel." Yet to some degree or other, every cup has the potential to be used for magick. In identifying your cup, you may feel drawn to elaborate, beautiful, expensive chalices. Don't be caught in this trap. Just because a cup is ornate or cost you dearly doesn't mean that it's the best one, the right one for you, or more magickal than another cup. Often it's the simple cups and handmade cups that most resonate for magickal work.

Spell 8: For Gathering Materials for Spells

YOU WILL NEED:

nutmeg

cinnamon

rosemary

bay leaves

peppercorns

five small containers to store the spices on your
   altar

Once you have an athame, a wand, a cup, a book of
shadows, and an altar to put them on, you'll want to start
collecting the materials you'll need to do spellwork in the
future. You'll start with a few items that will be helpful to
have, and then from time to time as you cast spells, you'll
add others. While you may think that you have to start
finding lurid items such as frog eggs and snake eyes to
cook in a cauldron, you won't need anything like them.
After you do this spell, you'll receive infrequent gifts that
are given to you by the natural world for especially potent
spellwork.

As you prepare for this spell, you'll want to get a few
items together that you'll keep on your altar for future
spells. You're starting to set up your supply of ingredients
and prepare yourself for finding more. Most kitchens will
have the spices just listed, and if not, they're easy to get at
any supermarket. You don't need a lot of each. Just a little
bit will be fine.

You'll also need containers for each of these spices, and
while they're important, they're not the primary focus of
this spell. You can get five all the same or five with a
theme (for example, jars that have different color tops on
the same body) or five each different from the others.
They don't need to be large. They do need to be secure

so that the spices won't fall out if the containers tip over by accident. Most craft stores sell small, unfinished wooden boxes which are perfect. You could also get inexpensive salt shakers. Leave them empty as you collect them because you'll fill them during the spell. These containers will stay on your altar, so you may want to find something that's a little nicer looking than a plastic bag, but it's totally up to you. Also, it's fine to use containers that are good enough for now and find better ones later. You can even cast a separate spell later on to call these containers to you.

This is a spell that enlists all your senses. You will use all of your senses to do the spell, and the spell will act on you to heighten your senses, which will enhance your magickal work from then on. Think about your five senses, taste, smell, touch, sound, and sight, as you prepare to do this spell.

The Spell: When all of the items are collected and put on your altar, ground and center. Cast the circle.

Stand in front of your altar, and say, "My altar is my sacred space, a place to keep and protect my sacred belongings." Think about your new tools and about how they're kept safely on your altar. And now think about the spices you're about to add to your altar. Although they aren't "tools" in the sense of hammer and nails, they're tools for casting spells.

Line up the spices in front of you, and have the containers nearby. Pick up the container of nutmeg. Look at the nutmeg, smell the nutmeg, feel a pinch of nutmeg, and, as you drop it back into its original container, listen to it. Think about how all these qualities of nutmeg are important. Now put a bit on your tongue and taste it. Notice how the taste stays with you for a while. Taste is what is really special about nutmeg. You're using nutmeg in this spell to be emblematic of all the tastes that your tongue is capable of discerning, one from the other. By including nutmeg in this spell, you're noting the importance of taste as one of your senses, and you're awakening your spiritual capacity to allow taste to affect your magick. Now put some in the new, special container, and say, "Nutmeg, you open my sense of taste."

Pick up the container of cinnamon. Look at the cinnamon, feel a pinch of cinnamon, and, as you drop it back into its original container, listen to it. Try tasting it. What is special about cinnamon, however, is the way it smells. Smell is a powerful sense. One whiff can bring back memories faster than any other sense. Think about how cinnamon connects you to your sense of smell and all the smells your nose can distinguish. Now put some in the new, special container, and say, "Cinnamon, you open my sense of smell."

Pick up the container of bay leaves. Look at the bay leaves. Smell them. Pick up one to feel it, and lick it to get its taste a little bit. Bay leaves are special because they sound different from other herbs when you crush them between your fingers. Crush some bay leaves and listen to the crinkles and snaps in your hands. Think about how bay leaves remind you of your sense of hearing and of all the sounds you can hear. Now put some in the new, special container, and say, "Bay leaves, you open my sense of hearing."

Pick up the container of rosemary. Smell the rosemary. Feel a pinch of it, and, as you drop it back into its original container, crush some and listen to it. Try tasting it. Rosemary is an interesting herb to look at. It's not usually a powder. It has a particular texture. Think about how this rosemary represents everything physical that you can see, and think about sight as a sense. By opening your inner spirit to this rosemary, you're heightening your ability to see what is physical, and at the same time, you're asking to increase your visual ability so that you can see into the inner nature of other beings and understand them better on a spiritual level. Decide that you'll pay more attention to all you see throughout the day, and that you won't take this important sense for granted. Now put some in the new, special container, and say, "Rosemary, you open my sense of sight."

Pick up the container of peppercorns. Look at it and carefully smell the peppercorn (try not to sneeze). Swirl it in its container and listen to it. Try tasting a tiny bit. Peppercorn kernels have an unusual feel to them. They're small, round spheres. In a way they're reminiscent of a miniature earth. Think about how pepper is characteristic of everything you touch and feel and how you do this throughout the day, mostly without paying any attention to it. Resolve to be more aware of each thing you touch and your sense of touch. Now put some in the new, special container, and say, "Pepper, you open my sense of touch."

Next, line up the newly filled containers, and put them on your altar with your other tools. Concentrate on how you have now heightened your senses. They're open so that in the future you'll have greater perception. The messages you'll receive are often subtle and seemingly unimportant, however, so you'll need to pay close attention to recognize them. For example, you may get a hunch that you should add basil to the spaghetti sauce you're making for dinner, even though you don't usually do that. This may be your body's inner voice directing you to connect spiritually with easing hatred or medicinally with easing digestion because this is what you'll need to make your next spell work well. Think of how you've attuned your body to be receptive to magickal messages from the spirit world.

Keeping all of this firmly in mind, say, "My body is my inner tool, and I have set up my altar with its magickal materials as an outward expression of my own inner altar."

These spices, along with your book of shadows, altar, athame, wand, and cup, are your new tools. They're the raw items you'll use to cast spells. But these new tools, your magickal materials, are the start of what will probably become a larger collection. Say, "May I receive more magickal materials as messages to use for the magick I will do and to guide me on the path I need to take." Envision yourself finding a feather on the ground. Envision finding part of an abandoned wasp nest. Envision yourself finding a seashell. Envision yourself finding a curl of birch bark that fell from a tree. Let these thoughts sink in for a moment, and then say, "May I recognize these gifts in whatever form they take as they come my way." Be attuned to all your senses to help you find these items and also to use these items in your spells.

Stand with your legs slightly apart so that you are very stable. Hold out your arms from your sides with your palms face up. Prepare yourself to receive energy, and when you're ready, say, "May I accept with grace magickal items from the earth to the sky and from the natural world filled with spirit, and may I receive the blessing of communication with the magickal world."

Devoke.

Magickal Wisdom: Magickal gifts come in unexpected ways and places.

The process of gathering objects for magickal work is ongoing. And as much as you're calling for objects to help with your spellwork, you're opening up yourself to recognize them when the spirit world puts them in your path. As long as you continue to work magick, you'll continue to find new objects for spells, usually just when you need them. In fact, when you find an unusual item, it'll become a clue for you to think about what's been on your mind and if the world is trying to encourage you to do magick or even to signal you that there's magick you need to do. What does your intuition say? One time I kept poking myself in the eye accidentally or bumping into things with my eye. After the third time I thought to myself, "What's going on that I keep sticking stuff in my eye? What a strange accident to have three times in one day." It turned out that I needed to pay attention to something I wasn't seeing straight (a particular kind of math problem we were learning that week), and this was a small way of being nudged to deepen my way of looking. Normally that's not the way I'd figure out math problems, but in this case, my test grade also sent a message to my teacher about what worked and what didn't in her teaching style for me; so it turned out that this message was multifaceted. She saw me, not as a lazy student, but as a student who responded better to instructions rather than examples. You'll probably also find other items when you least expect them. Some of the special items I've found include a broken bicycle pedal, a dried poppy seed case that I now use as a rattle, and a dead butterfly.

Spell 9: For Creating a Good Luck Talisman

YOU WILL NEED:

  3 strings: 1 white and 2 other colors (available at
    craft stores or some hardware or dollar stores)
  glue

Are you superstitious? Of course I'm not asking you to admit it, but face it, in the back of your mind, do you believe a little bit that wearing your favorite sweater will help you do better on your SATs? Me too. Whether or not you can prove that any superstitions are real, it's better to be safe than sorry. That's how I explain it to people who maintain they aren't superstitious. So here's how to create a special, magickal talisman that you can take with you everywhere.

Think about when you want to have this talisman. You will probably want to be able to take it to school, on dates, and on trips. You'll probably wear it all through the year. You're going to braid strings that you'll wear as a bracelet or anklet so that you can wear it when you don't have pockets. It'll be an object that other people will see without knowing about its special power.

Take the three strings. They should be sturdy and durable so that you can have this talisman for a long time. One will be white because this color purifies and intensifies other colors. One will be the color of your sun sign in the Zodiac. Choose yellow to symbolize Air if you are Gemini, Libra, or Aquarius. Choose red to symbolize Fire if you are Aries, Leo, or Sagittarius. Choose blue to symbolize Water if you are Cancer, Scorpio, or Pisces. Choose green to symbolize Earth if you are Taurus, Virgo, or Capricorn.

The third color will require some thought. You'll choose it, but it needs to reflect something personal about you. You might pick your favorite color. If you don't have a favorite color, you might choose the color of your favorite item in nature. Whichever color you choose, make sure that you have a specific reason for choosing it. It's fine if it duplicates one of the others you already picked. It'll just intensify the energy of that color in your spell.

The Spell: Ground and center. Cast your circle.

When you're between the worlds, stand tall in the center and breathe deliberately.

Have your three strings near you. Sit down, but try hard to keep your back straight as you do this work.

Pick up the white string, and say in a strong voice, "I start with white because of its purity."

Pick up the yellow, red, blue, or green string, and say, "I add (yellow, red, blue, or green) because I am a (state your Zodiac sign) and my inner light shines forth in this color."

Pick up the third string, and say, "I complete this triplet with (special color) because (here give your reason)."

Next knot the three strings together at one end. Begin to braid the three strings together, and as you do so, hum a tune to go with the words "luck for me" in a low tone. Keep thinking the words repeatedly in your head, and feel the vibration as you hum aloud.

When you're finished with the braiding, knot the other end. Put a little bit of glue on each knot to help the strings stay together. Blow on each one to help it dry, and as you blow, puff the air as if your breath were saying "Luck for me" in short bursts.

Choose whether you'll put the braid around your wrist or ankle. Is there a particular purpose for the luck you want? If it's something more foot oriented (perhaps you play soccer), then choose your ankle. If it's something more hand oriented (perhaps you're a painter so you choose the hand that holds your brush), then choose your wrist. Which will last longer? Which will be more comfortable to wear?

Next, stand in the center holding your braid. Say, "(Yellow, red, blue, green) reflects the sun that shines through me. (Your special color) resonates (the reason you chose this color). And white intensifies them both." Use a square knot to tie the braid onto your wrist or ankle, and say, "I increase my own power so that good luck finds me, follows me, accompanies me wherever I am and whatever I do." Now say, "It is so!"

Devoke, and end by stomping your feet three times.

Magickal Wisdom: Visualization is more than imagination.

Visualization combines all five senses in a sustained focus on something you want to happen in the future with the goal of making it come to pass. Imagination is a brief picture in your mind that could but most likely won't happen. Using your imagination, you could "see" what's to come in the future, but only in an uncontrolled way.

Visualization is a deliberate act to create the future by first having a mental image. While doing so, you should see, hear, feel, taste, and smell what you're visualizing. For example, if you're visualizing good luck for this talisman, feel the lucky energy circling your wrist or ankle, picture yourself receiving good luck (finding money, getting a good grade, and so on), and hear a voice saying you're lucky. Visualizing is important for mental control in all aspects of casting spells from the first grounding and centering meditation to calling the quarters and from collecting materials for the spell to grounding out the energy after saying, "So mote it be."

Adeptitude

Adeptitude is the opposite of ineptitude. Instead of complete incompetence, it means magickal mastery. I'm sure you never heard that word before because I made it up. That doesn't mean it's not real, it just means it's new.

You have gone between the worlds several times now, and you have returned with the new skill of casting a circle and also with a set of new tools. By the time you come to the end of this chapter, you'll have an athame, wand, cup, garment, and your book of shadows in hand to put on your altar. Still, you're probably skeptical about just how magickal that process was, and in truth you'll never completely leave that skepticism behind. You wouldn't be able to function in our *mundane* (non-magickal) world if you did. And while you have these tools in hand, you may wonder if they're truly magickal. Do you?

Rest assured, even if the process doesn't seem particularly magickal in hindsight, indeed magick brought your tools to you. By working in the sacred circle with your tools in these spells, you have started to recognize the spirit in everything around you.

In casting these spells you have given validity to a part of you that you may have previously squelched—your intuition. Many people do not like to admit that they pay attention to it in mundane life, but it is your greatest psychic power. The more you listen to it and follow it, the more magickal you will become as a person. You will find the spells you cast increasing in effectiveness. Every time you trust your intuition, you reinforce your willingness to walk in the spirit world.

What is your greatest psychic power?

Intuition. **Intuition is your greatest psychic power.**

But recognizing and listening to your intuition is only the beginning. You will also need to know the answer to the question: What is the most powerful force behind your spells? If you are ready, turn the page to become a dedicant.

CHAPTER 2

THE DEDICANT: SPELLS ABOUT BODY AND HEALTH

By NOW YOU'VE BEEN in sacred space and gathered tools. With the freedom to start at the very beginning without assumed knowledge or pretension, you've gotten some experience under your belt. Although you will always continue to ask questions, now you're ready to leave the role of seeker behind and dedicate yourself to trying magick. You may feel like, "Eh, so what? I haven't done much yet." Or you may feel like, "Hey, that was great! I want to do more!" And you may feel both of those at once. At any rate, you want to continue, and you're ready to make some changes happen.

As a *dedicant* you'll focus your energy on your physical body. You'll cast some spells that will fix problems and some that will prevent them. While casting these spells, you will work to bring yourself into balance physically, which is a positive side effect of spells related to the body. Although you may get excited about the changes you're making for other reasons, such as increasing your beauty or getting rid of pimples, the main one for starting with your physical body is that you use it to move energy. With a healthy and fit body, your magick will be stronger and more power-ful. It's also relatively easy to see the changes you're requesting. They'll happen relatively quickly, and the results will be clear. Of course, your body is already trying hard to make these changes to bring you into balance, but working magick in these spells will enhance your body's ability to heal or maintain your health.

You may not need to cast all these spells. Heck, if you're a guy, you'll definitely want to skip the two spells for women. And until you're sick, you won't need a spell to recover from a cold or flu. Even if you're not casting all the spells, read through them to understand them on a mental level. Try to do at least three if not five before moving on to the next chapter, "The Apprentice: Spells About School and Studying." Also, while you may be eager to move on, take your time and focus on the here and now of each spell. I recommend that you limit your magickal work to one spell per day. If you wait longer than that between spells, so much the better. You're giving yourself time to adjust magickally. This way you won't dis-sipate your energy; you'll put your full, concentrated force behind each one. Also, writing in your book of shadows about them is an excellent way to record your own notes about the spells and especially about the magickal wisdom.

In this chapter you're going to have a new meditation to ground and center and a new way to cast a circle. You'll notice that there are similarities to the way you did this in the first chapter, but there are also differences. Because you've had some practice, you're getting better at prepar-ing yourself and setting up sacred space to be between the worlds, and you'll notice that these two new methods will use your new proficiency. You'll be able to do this quickly, and it will make your spells more powerful.

Here is your grounding and centering meditation for the spells in this chapter. This method of grounding and centering involves sound. Try to concentrate on making really clear, steady sounds, and count slowly as you hold and release your breath. This will ground and center you with little effort. I've chosen sound because this chapter is about the physical aspect of your being. Sound is a way of making breath seem solid. It's not visible, but it has substance to it.

Grounding and Centering Meditation: The Sounds

Stand tall and straight, and take a deep breath.

Hold your breath for 4 seconds.

Exhale for 6 seconds making an "ah" sound as the breath comes out.

Take another deep breath and hold it for 4 seconds.

Exhale for 6 seconds making an "oo" sound as the breath comes out.

Take a third deep breath, and hold it for 4 seconds.

Exhale for 6 seconds, and make an "oh" sound as your breath comes out.

Take a moment to feel the center of your being and to feel your feet solidly on the ground. When you've done this deep breathing, proceed to casting the circle.

Here is how to cast the circle for the spells in this chapter. In this method of casting the circle, you'll use your new athame and wand. It's by casting the circle with them that you will begin to feel their energy. You will see how they help you direct and receive energy. By now, you've practiced setting up and working in a circle, and you'll also feel the circle that you created more strongly than before. The circle will be stronger because you'll be better at moving the energy and more practiced at sensing it as well.

Circle Casting: The Colors

Start in the north, and making each step purposeful, walk around your circle three times holding your athame close to your chest but pointing forward. Feel energy coming from your athame and visualize light coming from it that stays there as you walk forward. I like to visualize it at about hip height, but any height from floor to ceiling will work. Some people visualize it as a wall of light. It can be thin or thick, but whatever it looks like to you, it should be strong and impermeable. When you've finished, stop where you started in the north.

Put down your athame and pick up your wand.

Hold your wand in front of you with both hands close to your chest.

Start by standing quietly in the north. Then turn and face east; extend your hands out to hold your wand pointing up and down and call to the quarters.

In the east, say, "I call to East to welcome yellow Air."
Visualize the air as you say this.

Turn to the south, and say, "I call to South to welcome
red Fire." Visualize the fire as you say this.

Turn to the west, and say, "I call to West to welcome
blue Water." Visualize the water as you say this.

Turn to the north, and say, "I call to North to welcome
green Earth." Visualize the earth as you say this.

Your circle is cast.

The Spells

Spell 10: For Making a Pimple Disappear

YOU WILL NEED:

seeds in fruit (medium-size seeds work best)

You're lucky if you don't have acne, but you're not
human if you don't get pimples. No matter how much you
wash your face, inevitably you'll get a pimple when you
least want one and in the most embarrassing spot possible,
such as the end of your nose. Or maybe it'll be somewhere
that hurts, such as on the edge of your lip. You probably
already know not to pick at it because that will only make
the healing process longer. As you prepare to cast this
spell, think of the center of that pimple and of how you'll
start to heal around the pimple once that center is gone.

Make sure you have the right type of fruit with seeds
big enough to separate from the piece of fruit while it's in

your mouth. Perhaps you have watermelon or grapes with seeds in the kitchen already, but if not, go to your local market for some. Look carefully at the fruit, and pick one that will be ripe, sweet, and juicy because you're going to eat it. The size of the seeds is also important. A peach pit is too large, and strawberry seeds are too small.

The Spell: Ground and center. Cast the circle.

Remember that there are new ways to do these in this chapter. When you're between the worlds, stand in the north of your circle.

Hold the portion of fruit in front of you, and say, "Delicious fruit, I will consume you except for the inedible seeds." Then eat the fruit. It does not matter if you eat it in one bite or several, but you need to consume the full portion you put on your plate without removing any seeds from your mouth as you eat. That means you should be careful about the amount you choose to put on your plate because it would be difficult to eat a whole watermelon and especially difficult to do without swallowing or spitting out any of the seeds along the way. By the last bite, at least one seed should be in your mouth. When you are left with nothing but the seeds, spit out the seeds with great force. Shoot them across the room if you can. Make it a really powerful blast. Once out, say, "A pimple is like an unwanted seed that bears no fruit. Go out and stay away." Say, "My face will become restored to its original state. So be it."

Devoke, and end by clapping your hands three times.

Magickal Wisdom: Prepare for spells, and reinforce them with ordinary actions.

Magick works best when preceded and followed by mundane actions. A spell starts a change in motion in the spirit world, but mundane actions before and afterward support the change that's occurring in the physical world. Actions in the world are effective but in a different way from magick. Regular actions in the physical world are mundane because they're ordinary and recognizable even by people who don't practice magick. When you do something mundane in the physical world that relates to a spell before it is cast, you set the stage for the magick to work. When you do so after the spell is cast, you reinforce your magick. You add power by allowing the universe to open up more opportunities for your spell to become a reality. It's up to you, however, to recognize and take advantage of these opportunities that could be anything from a friend offering to lend a hand to a letter arriving in the mail with good news. As you do these mundane actions before or after the spell, be conscious of the magick that you plan to do or have done.

Spell 11: Against Acne

YOU WILL NEED:

water in your cup
salt
small piece of white paper
scissors
mirror

If you have acne, and I'm assuming you do since you're about to do this spell, your skin is out of balance and has been resistant to healing. Acne day in and out is the underbelly of raging hormones. As you prepare to do this spell, think about the fact that your skin is the largest organ in your body. Remember that skin is a membrane that acts as the frontline defense against germs and toxins that come into contact with your body. Acknowledge it as a protective layer that encapsulates your entire body, the bones and soft tissues. Skin is one of the most regenerative parts of your body. It works quickly to regrow where it has been broken.

The Spell: Ground and center. Cast your circle.

Sit down in the cross-legged position. Try to make yourself comfortable. Put your cup in front of you. Put a pinch of salt into the cup. Swirl the cup to mix in the salt. Take your athame, hold it with both hands around the handle, and point it into the water. Say, "I bless this water with its healing capacity. I charge it with healing energy. I call this water to aid me with its healing power."

Sit down with the paper in front of you. Cut it into a triangle shape that is small enough to fit into your cup without folding. Then use your mirror and burst one of your pimples. Choose one that's not too big so that the chances of it leaving a scar are small. Carefully squeeze the inside of the pimple so that the pus comes out. Put it on the center of the paper. Squeeze it all out to put as much of the pus as you can on the paper, but try not to get blood mixed up with what you put on the paper.

Put the triangle of paper down and concentrate again on your skin. When the pus on the paper is dry, which should only take a couple of minutes, put the paper into your cup. I know this process is gross, but it doesn't take long. And come on, can you honestly say that you never popped a pimple before?

Swirl your cup so that the water moves around in a counterclockwise direction. As you're doing this, say, "Salt water, bit of the sea, rinse this pus, and make me acne free!"

Devoke, and clap your hands to close the circle.

For the next three mornings when you get up, swirl the water in the cup in the same counterclockwise direction. You will notice that over time the pus will dissolve as the salt water washes it free, and your face will also heal.

Magickal Wisdom: Your subconscious guides you when you need it.

In your subconscious you know what is right for you even if your conscious mind can't recognize and articulate it. When you least expect it, like froth simmering up, you'll do something that you later realize was your subconscious guiding you when you were trying to suppress what was right for you. Your subconscious is also called your "little self" or "wise self" because deep down you have all the information you need. Accessing it is tough, and it takes most of us a lifetime to learn how to act on this guidance.

Do you ever seem to get in your own way? Everything is going along just fine, and then you do something stupid to screw up your plans. Well, at least that's how it works for me. But usually I find that I was actually steering myself back to my own center, what's right for me. One time I was dating a guy I was crazy about, but I ended up annoying him so that he broke up with me. I was heartsick. Secretly I'd thought I might marry him. In retrospect, he was totally wrong for me. He thought my spellcraft was baloney, and while some people wouldn't care, he would've been a terrible partner for me because I do care. Still, it was important for me to see how my inner compass guided me and to learn from it.

Spell 12: Against Weight Problems

YOU WILL NEED:
  modeling clay
  20 or more coins
  stick
  orange candle
  matches

Weight is a weighty matter when it comes to your self-image. Your body is your physical manifestation in the world, the part of you that everyone else sees. People only get to know the inner you after interacting with you. Because your body gives a first impression, you want to look good, and if you are too fat or thin, you can feel self-conscious.

As you prepare for this spell, keep in mind that your body has an ideal range for your weight. Hormones regulate your weight, and with exercise, diet, and proper care, you can adjust it. Concentrate on your ability to change your body's shape, fitness, and size.

Modeling clay comes in many colors and styles. You can easily find it at a craft or art supply store. Clay that does not need to be baked will be less of a hassle than the type that does, especially clay that needs to be fired in a kiln. You'll need 4 ounces or more in order to make two disks about 4 inches in diameter. They need to be thick enough for you to carve a symbol in them using the stick.

You will need an even number of coins. Try to have twenty or more, but whichever coin you choose, make sure that all of them are the same type. Other than that, it doesn't matter if they're pennies, nickels, dimes, quarters, or Spanish doubloons, if you have them.

Look for an orange candle. Orange signals and triggers adaptability, so it will encourage the change you want in your body. If you cannot find an orange candle, use a white candle, and peel an orange so that a large portion of the peel comes off in one strip. You can then curl the peel around the white candle.

The Spell: Ground and center. Cast the circle.

Light the candle, and keep in mind the change you want in your body.

Sit down in front of your altar and take out the modeling clay. Work it in your hands so that it becomes the same warm temperature as your hands. Then divide it in half so that you have two lumps the same size. Shape each of these into a slightly concave disk about 4 inches wide (make sure they're flat enough to stack items on them because you're going to put the coins in them later). When you've finished both of them, they should be about the same size, thickness, and shape, and they should look like the dishes in a scale used for weighing objects but without the cords to hang them from a central standard.

When you have made the two disks, pick up the stick and draw a five-pointed star in each. This star is called a *pentacle* (when it is in a circle it is called a *pentagram*), and it's a symbol of the human body, which is precisely what you want to change.

Place the disks on your altar side by side, and pick up the coins in your hands. Coins are also associated with the north in part because you can use them to buy objects. Cupping your hands around the coins, say, "I charge these coins to decrease my weight as I remove them." Stack an even number on each disk. (If you are looking to gain weight, say "add" instead of "remove" and "increase" instead of "decrease," and stack only one coin on each disk. Keep the others in a container on your altar.)

Still sitting, say, "My body has the amazing ability to change as I will it. Over the upcoming days the scales will get lighter (heavier if you're trying to gain weight)." End by saying, "So mote it be," and blow out the candle.

Devoke.

Over the course of the next five or more days, remove one coin from each of the two piles daily. Put the coins outside, either in a body of water or by a tree trunk. Do not spend this money. As far as you're concerned, these coins are no longer valuable as money. They have far greater magickal value. It's fine to dispose of them this way each day or all at once as long as you remove them from the scales on your altar daily.

If you did the spell for gaining weight, add a coin to the top of each pile daily until they're all stacked on the scales. When you're done, dispose of them the same way as if the spell had been for gaining weight, except that you will dispose of them all at once rather than taking them outside in pairs daily.

Magickal Wisdom: The natural world preserves an order of balance.

Maintaining balance in your body will promote balance in your life, which will in turn enable you to work with magick accurately. In nature, ecosystems consist of thousands of plants and animals in the various stages of their cycles of life. That concept is extraordinary to think about, and one small change can unbalance the entire ecosystem. But here's the remarkable thing: it will work to get back to that original balance. Your body is like a fragile ecosystem. You have to maintain not only your physical shape but also your emotional and spiritual sides as well. Do your best to preserve your own balance in your body and in your life and in the world around you. The less stress your body has, the more effective your magick will be. To get grounded and centered or stay that way is hard when you're imbalanced, but the balance you have when you're grounded and centered will increase your magick's precision.

Spell 13: Against Bad Hair

YOU WILL NEED:

 your hairbrush

 comb

Whether you have "bed head" when you wake up in the morning or "hat head" during the day, sometimes you need help for your hair to look good.

While you may think of your hair as a single body part, your scalp actually has thousands of individual hairs on it. The way you wear your hair, be it in a short coif or a long ponytail, is really a way to gather these individual hairs to look as if they're one part of your body. When you think about it this way, it's a wonder you don't have more trouble with your hair. As you begin this spell, think of each individual hair coming together in an organized way on your head.

The Spell: Ground and center. Cast the circle.

When you're between the worlds, stand in the center, and say, "Hair, I address you as an important part of me." Sitting down as you cast this spell is okay as long as you make sure that your back is straight.

Pick up your brush, and begin to brush your hair making strokes all the way from your scalp to the end of your hair. Do this for a few minutes. You should feel relaxed and calm. Put aside all your matted hair woes for now.

Use your fingers to pull some of the snarled hair from your brush. Get a bunch of it out and put the tangle on your altar. Take out your athame, point the athame right into the tangle, and say, "Hair, I send energy to you to make you straighten your tangles." Take a deep breath and exhale slowly while still holding your athame in the tangle.

Put down your athame, and pick up the tangle pinched between your finger and thumb. Start combing through the tangle in a methodical way. The comb should go through the tangle gently, pulling the hair straight as it goes. It's not necessary to make long strokes through it. Try little strokes at first. The idea is to untangle it as well as you can (you don't have to be perfect!) without breaking the strands. Be careful as you work, but keep concentrating on the tangle becoming straight, and as you do so, think of the hair on your head also becoming free of tangles.

Take a moment and imagine yourself on a beach or a boat or a high cliff, anywhere that's windy. Imagine how nice it feels to have the wind blow your hair and how especially great it is to have your hair stay neat and tangle free even when the wind is in your hair.

When you have the tangle as straightened as you're going to get it (untangled with free strands of hair), open your window, and blow it outside. As you breathe out to blow it away, visualize a tangle transformed to tamed hair as a gift for the wind.

Finally, say, "May the wind always be a friend to my hair and keep it looking its best."

Devoke and end by nodding your head vigorously so that you are flipping your hair up and down in a whipping motion three times and visualizing the energy of the circle flowing back into the earth each time you flip down.

Magickal Wisdom: Magick prefers that you use the easiest method first.

That means that if there is a mundane solution, try that first. This doesn't mean that you shouldn't do the spell because you've taken action in the mundane world such as washing your hair and putting conditioner in it regularly. Go ahead and do the spell for reinforcement. I mean, why take chances when you can be sure? But the path of least resistance will get the fastest and most effective results. Work on your hair by brushing it, washing it, adding gel, or blowing it with a drier before doing the spell.

Spell 14: For Diminishing PMS

YOU WILL NEED:

raspberry tea

a mug for a hot beverage (preferably your magickal cup)

If you feel as if you spend much too much time dealing with the bloating, aching, and grouchiness of premenstrual syndrome (PMS), this spell will help balance your body and mind during this uncomfortable time.

Raspberry tea bags are easy to find at many supermarkets or from health food stores. Get a package of this tea. Raspberry has long been known as a folk remedy to tone the uterus and to decrease the pain of menstrual cramps. The leaves are what have the strong curative power, but the fruit makes it taste good. PMS makes you cranky. Nothing soothes like a warm cup of tea, and as you brew it, think about how much this spell is going to help.

This spell will encourage your natural beauty to come forth. Physical beauty isn't about sexy clothes and expensive jewelry, it's about a person's shape and proportions.

As you prepare to do this spell, recognize that each person radiates beauty in a different way. I know you've heard that before, and you're probably saying to yourself, "But I need something different—not some speech." This spell will affect your physical being, not just the inner beauty that all of us are capable of attaining through kindness and compassion.

As you gather your materials, think about how you could be beautiful. Don't think that you have to be a blonde when you're a brunette. Try to focus your energy on what your best features are. Recognize your problematic features. Keep them all in mind without judging them.

The Spell: Ground and center. Cast the circle.

Stand tall and reach your arms up to the ceiling. Breathe deeply and let it out slowly. Feel your body stretched tall and thin.

Then sit down, and cut your piece of paper into a round shape. Decorate the paper as a flower with petals. Any type of flower that you like is fine. You can use magic markers, colored pencils, pastels, and so on. You can cut a flower out of a catalog and glue it on in a collage method. As you create this flower, continually think about enhancing your good physical features and improving your problematic physical features. Even if your "bad" features seem as if they can't change, whether they're ears that stick out or feet that are extra large, this spell will help change those features and help your other features compensate for them. The changes may seem imperceptible, but they're happening. You may not notice a difference because usually these changes happen at a cellular level over time, but later a friend may ask if you got a new haircut or lost weight. For example, if you have large feet, this spell might make your feet a little smaller while increasing the water retention in your legs and ankles to make your feet seem more proportionate.

When you've finished it, stand tall again and reach your hands up while holding the flower between both hands so that the flower part is facing up to the sky. Say, "May the beauty of the sky fill my flower." Then squat down and press the face of the flower to the floor. Say, "May the beauty of the earth transform my flower." Next, take some water, and wet the back of the flower. Lift or remove your shirt, and press it against your chest so that it sticks on you. While it's on you, it's transferring its beauty into you. Say, "I accept the beauty of the sky and earth in my body." Leave the flower on you until it falls off. Depending on the kind of paper, it may stay on for a while or it may stay on for only a few seconds. The length of time isn't important. The skin-to-flower contact can happen in an instant or slowly. Let it do its work.

When you're done, devoke. Rip the flower into bits and sprinkle them onto the floor as you ground the circle's energy.

Magickal Wisdom: Energy moves through your body best when you are properly aligned.

Stand and sit up straight. Do not slouch or sag or droop. I mention this now because this spell involves sitting down. In the beginning of a spell, it's easy to remember to sit with a straight back, especially after casting the circle and breathing deeply. But then while sitting, you can easily forget that and start to slouch. Stop it as soon as you notice it and realign. Your spell will work better if you do because a straight body can move more energy more effectively than a slouched body. Does this sound like the familiar advice to stand up straight that you hear from parents and teachers? That's because this advice about the magickal world applies to the ordinary world too.

Spell 17: For Keeping a Straight Face

YOU WILL NEED:

old deck of cards

thick black permanent marker

glue

This is the poker face spell. In the game of poker, it's important not to let your face give away secret information to your opponent. After all, there's usually something valuable at stake. You may not have money on the table, but a straight face can be your ally when you need it. So as you prepare, think of all the different muscles in your face and parts of your face. Be hypersensitive to the huge number of ways that your face can move. Keeping your muscles from moving is hard even for a short time. But you start by being conscious of each part of your face.

Find an abandoned deck of cards that you won't miss. You're going to make it useless anyway in terms of playing cards during this spell. Also, get a thick black permanent marker.

The Spell: Ground and center. Cast the circle.

When you're between the worlds, sit down and hold your pack of cards in one hand. Take a deep breath, and let it out slowly onto the cards.

Pull out the four aces, one for each suit, hearts, diamonds, clubs, and spades. Also, pull out a joker. Say, "My straight face will protect me." On the back of each card, draw a smiley face that isn't smiling or frowning (two dots for eyes and a straight line for the mouth). The aces stand for purity, and each suit corresponds to one of the four directions, so you are invoking the elements to aid you. Then rip the joker card into five pieces. Glue one piece of the torn joker card to each of the ace cards on the side of the card with the ace on it, not the back of the card where you put the straight face.

Stand up, and say, "Jokers in life, your powers will not affect me. When I need a straight face, the power of the elements will protect me." Carry the cards with you in either a pocket or bag (handbag, tote, backpack, and so forth) from now on.

Devoke, and throw the fifth piece of the joker card on the floor. Stomp your foot on the joker piece as you ground the energy of the circle.

Magickal Wisdom: Magick and drugs do not mix.

A straight face is useful in life, but staying straight is imperative. Drugs and alcohol alter your physical body. In fact, they're about as good a combination with magick as drinking and driving, so leave them behind. Intoxicants will just mess up your magick. It's true that shamans in indigenous tribes have used various drugs to induce trances. But naturally occurring substances aren't as strong as what's sold on the street. Also in tribal cultures taking these drugs is considered dangerous and only done when absolutely necessary. Shamans acknowledge the poison within these substances by noting the initial stages of vomit, diarrhea, and other unpleasantness. You don't need that type of experience, and you definitely don't need the law coming after you.

Spell 18: For Getting Over a Cold or Flu

YOU WILL NEED:

stiff white paper
scissors
pen or magic marker
green, white, or brown candle

You are probably sniffling, blowing your nose, sneezing and coughing, and feeling downright miserable as you gather materials for this spell. Take a moment to think of all your symptoms, but try not to dwell too much on how they make you feel.

I suggest that you use stiff, white paper, but any paper will do. As you choose your candle, think of the element Earth and of how these three colors relate to it: brown for dirt and bark, green for grass and leaves, and pure white for snow.

The Spell: Ground and center. Cast the circle.

Rest for a moment between the worlds before starting the spell. It takes energy to set up sacred space, and you want to give yourself a brief amount of time to gear up for the spell.

Sit calmly in the center of your circle. Take your scissors and cut the white paper into a circle larger than the bottom of your candle. Next, draw a pentagram on the paper. A pentagram is a five-pointed star that has a circle whose rim touches each of the five points on the star. Put the paper with the pentagram down, and sprinkle a pinch of cinnamon on the pentagram. Then put the candle on top of it. If you're feeling sick and need to go slowly, it's fine to rest as you need to.

Imagine all your aches and pains, all the mucus, and everything that's part of this sickness dissipating by flowing down into the ground. Then hold the candle so that both of your hands are on it. Stare at the candle and picture your body as it is when it is whole and healthy, when it feels great. Channel those thoughts into the candle to charge it with your own healing energy and vision of wellness. Sprinkle more cinnamon on top of the candle. Here you're using cinnamon because it's the spice associated with your sense of smell. You're probably not using your nose much with this cold, but the cinnamon will help you regain your ability to breathe through your nose and smell.

Light the candle, and say, "Earth, quicken my healing process, and transform my body to wellness." Let the candle burn down.

Devoke.

Drink a lot to let toxins flow out of your body, and get plenty of sleep to recuperate. Remember that the best medicine of all is to take care of yourself in a mundane, preventative way by getting enough sleep, drinking plenty of water, eating nutritiously, and doing all the other things that you know you should to take care of yourself. If you have not been taking those steps, resolve to do so once you recover from this bout.

Magickal Wisdom: Staying healthy and avoiding stress promote effective magick.

If you're not well physically, then you're not in top form to work magick. Sickness contributes to making it harder for you to work magick and have the magick be effective. This spell is purposefully simple so that it has the best chance of getting good results with little effort from you. Your body naturally wants to be in the best health possible. I find that it takes double the energy when I'm sick to make a spell work well.

Adeptitude

You are wielding your tools to cast spells. Where before, the changes you summoned in your spells seemed ethereal, in this chapter you changed something physical—your body. You may not have realized that you had such immense power to make these changes. Losing a few pounds is one matter, and giving a new appearance to your body is another.

By casting these spells, you have set in motion changes at the cellular level in your body. Each spell you've cast in this chapter has charged your body with the readiness to change more than the spell before it. Why is this?

Whether or not you thought about it before, there is a powerful current running through your body. That is right, energy. The electrical current within you makes your heart beat and gives you a shock when you touch an electrical outlet. Energy charges your body, and you direct that energy each time you unleash it in casting a spell.

What is the most powerful force behind spells?

Your energy. **Your personal energy is the most powerful force behind spells.**

From now on your ability to cast spells will improve as you become more adept at directing energy. But intuition and energy are not all there is to casting effective spells. You will need to find out: What is your most important tool of all? Will you move forward to learn the lessons of the apprentice to find out?

CHAPTER 3

THE APPRENTICE: SPELLS ABOUT SCHOOL AND STUDYING

WITH SEVERAL SPELLS under your belt, you're more familiar with magick. And now you're more serious too. At this level, you become an apprentice. You've gone through the initial introductory stage of questioning and deciding to dedicate. You'll always have a bit of every stage with you, but now you can focus your attention on where your path is going without stopping so frequently to wonder if this is the path for you.

Previously, you've cast spells that related to starting work in the magickal world by concentrating on your space, tools, and yourself alone. This chapter gives you a big jump because these spells focus on school which is a place in your life where you're surrounded by other people. Most can be done at home while you're privately in your sacred space, but they affect your studying and time at school. Once again, I recommend that you read through all the spells to understand them even if there are spells that you don't need to cast right away. You can always go back later on and cast the spells when you need them.

The spells in this chapter will help you do well in your classes and will protect your computer, your locker, and you when you're in the cafeteria. There're also a couple of spells to keep you out of trouble. Although there're many people around you in school, it's not until the last two spells in this chapter that you'll work any magick involving other people. These spells won't involve specific people, and you'll learn why it's important to keep it that way. As you progress, you'll see that some of the magickal wisdom selections relate to each other or that one builds on another. It's important to keep all the wisdom selections in mind even if you haven't cast all the spells. Perhaps you will notice other areas of your life that demonstrate their wisdom but seem unrelated to your spellcraft. If you take some time to consider what happened, you'll see that they're related. All areas of life are connected even if they don't seem so now. Magick has a way of bringing up personal issues when you need to address them, although usually it feels like the worst timing possible. This process is often hard; however, it will make you stronger.

Here is your grounding and centering meditation for the spells in this chapter. You've had some practice with the grounding and centering meditations in the last two chapters, and now you'll learn a similar yet more advanced one for this new phase of magick in this chapter. You'll feel more confidence in your ability to slow your body down and to be aware of each part of it. Take your time as you prepare to make the transition to sacred space.

Grounding and Centering Meditation: The Whole Body

Align your back so that each vertebra sits squarely on the one below it. Breathe deeply. Plant your feet so that you feel each part of them on the ground. Be aware of the balls of your feet, your toes, your heels, and your arches hovering above.

Next, feel your ankles, your calves and shins, your knees, your thighs. Continue moving up through your hips and waist, being conscious of each part of your body as you go. Feel your ribs, your chest, your sides.

Continue up to your shoulders and down your arms to feel your biceps and triceps, elbows, forearms, wrists, and palms, and out to your fingers. Feel your neck in front and back, feel your chin, your mouth, your nose, ears, eyes, and forehead, and feel the top of your head.

Feel each individual part of your body, and also be aware of your whole body at the same time. When you feel both at the same time, you are ready to commence your magickal work.

Here is how to cast the circle for the spells in this chapter. Different animals correspond to each of the four quarters, and you will call to the spirit of each animal to stand guard at the edge of your circle. When all four are in place, your sacred space is safe and balanced. Animals are a longtime favorite for catching the essence of the four quarters because it's easy to imagine an animal, its color, movement, and size as being representative of the protection you're calling into your circle. The animals may also seem to have a closer connection to the quarters because they spend time there. For example, birds fly, so they spend a lot more time in the air than people do. But people have a connection with air, too, as you know from holding onto your hat on windy days.

Circle Casting: Animals

Hold your athame with your dominant hand and point it toward the north. Hold your nondominant hand open and facing forward behind the athame so that the end of the athame's handle touches the palm of your nondominant hand. Walk from north to east and pause, east to south and pause, south to west and pause, and west to north again. As you do this, imagine a laser ray from the tip of your athame leading the way around the circle. Do this a second time, but do not pause at each quarter. Then do it a third time more boldly yet. Put down your athame and get your wand.

Then walk to face each direction starting silently in the north.

Turn to the east, and say, "Eagle, I see you approach, soaring in the sky."

Turn to the south, and say, "Salamander, I see you
approach crawling on hot rocks."
Turn to the west, and say, "Dolphin, I see you
approach swimming through the ocean."
Turn to the north, and say, "Bear, I see you approach
bounding through the meadow."
The animals' spirits are protecting your circle, and you
can work magick safely.

The Spells

Spell 19: For Protection in the Cafeteria

YOU WILL NEED:

dry cracker

paper napkin

The cafeteria can be a separate hazard zone at school,
but here is help to protect you from difficult situations
during lunch.

As you prepare for this spell, think of the cafeteria as
the place where food is prepared, served, and eaten. That's
its main function. And there's a long history of people cel-
ebrating by eating together. We're social eaters who gather
together and share food as opposed to other animals such
as lions and dogs who are competitive eaters as demon-
strated by their fighting each other for food and eating in
a hierarchical order.

Find a dry cracker. Saltines are a fine example. And get
a fairly large paper napkin.

The Spell: Ground and center. Cast the circle.

Stand in the center of the circle, unfold your napkin, and lay it flat on the floor. Think of all the embarrassing and negative situations that can happen in the cafeteria. You cannot find a seat. The only place to sit is with kids who hate you. The food tastes like cardboard, is unrecognizable, and makes you sick. Think of all these awful situations. Take a deep breath, let it out, and say, "Yuuuuhhhhhhk." (That's yuck made into a long tone.)

Put the cracker in your mouth and chew. As you chew it, concentrate on all that negativity. Do not swallow it! Chew and chew, and when it's completely mushy, get down on all fours and spit the half-eaten food into the napkin. Visualize all that bad energy going with it into the napkin. Plunk, it lands outside of you. Say, "Pttooooey!"

Wad up the napkin into a tight ball and hurl it into your garbage can. Devoke, and don't look at the napkin again.

Magickal Wisdom: Harm none.

"Harm none" is the first part of the Wiccan Rede that says, "An it harm none, do what you will." It's a major law for people working magick. In the world of magick, it's fine to do whatever you want as long as you're not hurting anybody, intentionally or unintentionally. It's relatively easy to think and figure out a way around intentional harm, although it's harder to get around the broiling emotions that make you want to cause harm. Take a step back. This is a powerful law—harm none—and you'd be much better off if you heed it. Nobody can stop you from doing something; you have to refrain from it yourself. It's harder to avoid unintentional harm. You'll learn more about this later (it's called "manipulative magick"). It's also important to realize that harm none includes you. You can't do magick that will cause yourself harm. Probably you wouldn't do that intentionally, but it does mean that you have to think hard about each spell before casting it to avoid creating problems for yourself. Most of us live by this advice anyway in our day-to-day lives, but while working with magick, it's helpful to keep it in the forefront of one's mind.

Spell 20: Against Falling Asleep in Class

YOU WILL NEED:

thin yellow string
small jingle bell with a loop so that it can be put on a
    string (available at craft stores)

Whether you're filling a requirement by taking a class that you'd rather not have to attend or you just have a teacher who speaks in a monotone and finds minute details exciting, you must pass this class. In order to do that, you have to absorb enough of the course material to show "mastery" of the subject.

Concentrate on staying awake, alert, and attentive in classes that are particularly boring as you find the string and bell you need. There may be something interesting about the subject, but you don't know what it is, and the teacher only seems to make it worse rather than bringing the subject to life. Think about how that subject must be interesting to someone in the world, otherwise there wouldn't be teachers in that subject. (Consider that your teacher is an adult who decided to spend his or her life dedicated to teaching that subject in school.)

If you cannot find yellow string, find white string and a yellow magic marker with a wide tip. Just run the marker over the string to make it yellow. The string should be about twelve inches long, but this will depend on the thickness of the string. You can test how much string each knot uses by measuring a piece of string, making a knot, then measuring again and subtracting the difference. (Make sure you remove any practice knots so that your string is straight when you start the spell.) Make the string longer than you think you'll need so you can cut it to the right size during the spell. The bell should be small but should have a loop so that the string fits through it. And of course you should like the sound of it. For this spell I like a dull tone so that it doesn't cause too much attention in class.

The Spell: Ground and center. Cast the circle.

First pick up the jingle bell and look at it. Shake it a little bit to hear its sound. Spend a moment appreciating the way a bell's sound rings you back to the present from any daydreaming. Then put the bell down.

Take a deep breath and let it out slowly. Think about those boring classes and how there must be something interesting about them. Concentrate on finding that interesting nugget of information. Sit down and tie a knot two inches from one end of the string. I suggest a square knot (left over right then right over left). The knots should be nubbly and stick out as bumps in the string. Keep your focus on finding the interesting key to the subjects. Tie a second knot one inch from the first. Add the small jingle bell onto the string and put a third knot one inch from the second knot with the bell tied tightly in the third knot. Tie a fourth knot an inch from the third and a fifth knot an inch from the fourth. Last cut the string so that there are two inches on the end (the same length as the other end). Your knotted string should be about nine inches long. Now crumble some bay leaves over the string with its knots and bell. As you do this you're heightening its ability to trigger your hearing since its your spice associated with sound and hearing.

Hold the knotted string with one end in each hand. Exhale onto the string. Say, "Inspire me to find the interesting core in my classes."

Devoke, and stomp your feet five times to ground the energy.

Wear this string of knots as a bracelet during your boring classes. The bell will make noise and wake you up just when you are losing your focus or when the teacher is covering something important in class.

Magickal Wisdom: Magick is real.

Perhaps it seems strange to read this as a special lesson when you're reading a whole book about magick. Why would there be a book about it if it weren't real? It's real, and it's important to read that and say it to yourself every so often because there are people who don't agree. What you need to know is that magick is subtle. Rarely does lightning flash and a change happen instantaneously. It's hard for the world to maintain balance when change is violent and eruptive. Changes from spells often happen gradually so that you don't see progress as it's happening, or the changes from spells occur in a way that you weren't expecting. This bracelet with the bell on it will ring and call your attention back to class, and you'll notice that usually it rings at precisely the time that you need to know something for the class. That's its special magick. In addition, there will be something about what you learned that interests you personally and relates to something in your life outside of this class. You've charged this bracelet with the power to do this, and although you may not recognize it as it's happening, later on you'll probably realize why that bell jingled when it did.

Spell 21: For Late-Night Energy

YOU WILL NEED:
   sage stick
   feather
   matches
   aluminum foil (a nonflammable surface used
      to catch falling ashes)
   oil

This is the night owl spell. Maybe you have to write a term paper, maybe you have to pull your entire science project together in one night, or maybe you are facing exam cram, but you want to avoid chugging coffee or super-caffeinated soda when staying up late. You need to have enough energy to focus on what you are doing when the subject seems to be more sleep inducing than a sleeping pill. An owl is awake at night naturally. Think about owls as their senses heighten at night in preparation for their search for food. When you do this spell, you borrow the power of the owl to stay awake with that same keen focus.

Your nonflammable surface could be anything including an actual cauldron, a metal pot from the kitchen, or a piece of aluminum foil. Since aluminum foil is readily available and easy to dispose of, that's what I've listed here. I recommend that you use a feather that you've found outside while walking around. It's best if it comes from an owl, but if not, that's okay too. The oil should be something astringent such as peppermint or eucalyptus, smells that open your nasal passages if you have a cold.

The Spell: Ground and center. Cast the circle.

Put your aluminum foil in the center of the circle. Take out your sage, and hold it in front of you. Think of the owl and its special power to hunt at night. Put the sage down on the aluminum foil. Hold your arms stretched out to the side like wings. Close your eyes and feel the wind whooshing by your arms as if you were flying in the air. Pretend that you are high in the air in the dark night and "look" down at the ground. (Do all of this with your eyes closed!)

Open your eyes and pick up the sage. Light it and blow out the flame so that it has a smoking ember at the end. Take the feather and gently waft the smoke toward you. This is called "smudging." Breathe in the smell of the smoke. Having the smoke gently touch your body and clothes while you breathe deeply is a way of purifying yourself outside and in. Say, "Owl, I become you. I receive your nighttime gift. My awareness is now keen, and I am ready to stay focused."

Smell the strong, minty oil and anoint yourself with it on the middle of your forehead. Say, "I am part of the night. I have become awakened to the power of being alert in the dark."

Devoke.

Magickal Wisdom: Synchronicity is your magickal tool.

Coincidence is an act of two or more unplanned things happening at the same time. Synchronicity is an act of two or more unplanned things happening at the same time for a reason. As you work magick, you'll notice that usually coincidences are really messages to you from the spirit world. It's nature's way of winking at you and telling you to take notice. If you have a gut feeling, that twinge deep inside you is saying you should pay attention. It can tell you if danger is near or if you're getting yourself into trouble. Often we shrug our shoulders and ignore these warnings. We dismiss these feelings as mere coincidences. But once you're working with magick, this is the world's way of reinforcing a message to you. You have to fine-tune yourself, however, to notice these messages. They're there if you look, but most people discard these signs as irrelevant in their lives. Of course they're relevant, and it's up to you to figure out how.

Spell 22: Against Difficult Homework

YOU WILL NEED:

stick of soft butter
knife
stone

During this spell, you're going to cut through difficulty despite your need to master difficult concepts, to read long passages, or to write articulate papers. Think about the heap of homework you have and about how you want to cut it down to size. Think about organizing it into sections so that the big load seems like many little sections, each of which is easy and short to do.

In addition to your athame, you're going to use a regular knife for this spell. Choose one that is comfortable to use and silently ask its permission to take part in your ritual before bringing it to your circle. The butter should be soft, so take it out of the refrigerator and let it warm a bit. Don't melt it in a pan. You need it to be in stick form on a plate of some sort. You need a stone that fits in the palm of your hand.

The Spell: Ground and center. Cast the circle.

When you're between the worlds, put the stick of butter on the plate (if it isn't there already), and hold the plate with both hands. Breathe on it. Put it down, and pick up your athame. Holding it with both hands, put the tip of the athame's point into the butter, and use a strong voice to say, "I will ease my homework load."

Stand with your legs apart, and say, "My homework seems so great a task, but I can cut through it like butter." Pick up the knife (not your athame), and cut the butter in half once. It should be very easy to do, so concentrate on how easy it is. Then say, "My homework is manageable, it decreases as I work," and cut each half of the stick of butter into half again (so there are four pieces total). Then say, "My homework is easy and done quickly," and cut each quarter into half so that you have eight pieces. Using your athame, carve an 8 into each one so that they look like Spanish pieces of eight coins.

Then pick up the eight pieces of butter one at a time and rub at least some of each one around the stone. As you do so, say, "Before me I have pieces of eight, pirates' treasure, unexpected money, and I spend these eight golden pieces on easing my homework. It's a small cost for something so great." Think about how an 8 on its side is the mathematical symbol for infinity and how your homework will be infinitely easier after this spell.

Devoke, and end by making three small jumps in which you land heavily on both feet.

Take the buttery stone outside, and put it next to a tree.

Magickal Wisdom: Look for patterns in life.

Life has patterns for a reason. People look for patterns and meaning in life to make sense of the world around

them. That is human nature. Some meaning is super-
imposed by humans on events, and some is truly valid.
Nobody can tell you which is which. You will have to distinguish that for yourself, and this is one of the hardest
abilities to develop while working magick. I will say that
sometimes you won't get exactly what you asked for, but
you will get what you need. At first, you may think the
spell didn't work. Open your mind and consider recent
events carefully. If you consider the situation closely, there
is a reason why you got these results. After casting this
spell, you may end up with more homework, but it's easier
and faster for you to do. You may end up with less homework, but something new to learn about. Look for how
this spell affected your workload, and then look for the
meaning. Why do you think the spell did that? There is
a reason, a pattern in life if you look closely. It is only a
matter of figuring out what it is.

Spell 23: For Protecting Your Computer Files

YOU WILL NEED:
   square of white paper
   blue pen

Nothing is more frustrating than spending a lot of time
writing a paper or other project on your computer and then
losing all your work. Even if you remember to save your
files frequently, you can lose your hard drive. This talisman
will have the specific purpose of protecting your computer
files by honoring the force that records all information in

computers—binary. Binary is a counting system in base two. That means there are only two digits, zero and one or on and off.

As you prepare, think of how you want your information on your computer files to be safe and preserved. Think of your computer as your personal stronghold. Concentrate on what important information needs protection yet easy access. Cut a piece of paper into a perfect square. Any size with sides between three and six inches long will be fine.

You need two types of protection: the first is protection from people who shouldn't have access to your private information, and the second is from mishaps such as computer crashes and failing technology. If you want protection from people, add passwords and store your files on external disks that you carry with you. Computer crashes are a bigger problem and, therefore, the focus of this spell because they mean that you cannot get to your own material. As an aside, it does mean that nobody else is going to get that information either.

The Spell: Ground and center. Cast the circle.

Sit down cross-legged, but with a straight back. Put your hands on your knees with your palms facing up. Sit and breathe for a moment. Inhale, and as you exhale say "One" in a voice with a tone to it. Try to make the word last at least four seconds long. Inhale again, and as you exhale say "None" using a tone as if it is a long, slow chant. As you speak each of these syllables, think about how similar they are in sound. They both have only one syllable and rhyme. Yet one of them represents presence and the other absence. Continue with this chant until you feel calm, relaxed, and in tune with the binary forces that drive computers.

Take out the square of paper and put it on the floor. Press your hands, palms down, on the square. Your hands may be larger than the paper, and that's okay. Make sure that an equal amount from each hand is touching the paper. Visualize energy coming out of your dominant hand, going through the paper, and flowing down into the earth. Once you're doing that with ease, add your nondominant hand by visualizing energy flowing from the ground, up through the paper, and into your nondominant hand. Keep doing this so that you have a circle of energy flowing out from your body through your dominant hand, through the paper, down into the earth, and up again through the paper into your nondominant hand. Once again, chant "One" and "None" while concentrating on how one means the presence of something and none means the absence of something. Do this at least three times, preferably a bit longer until you really get into a rhythm with it.

Then on the paper square, draw a square, and divide it into quarters so that there are four smaller squares within the bigger square. In the top left square write 1 and in the top right square write 0. Then in the bottom left square write 0 and in the bottom right square write 1. Hold the paper in your hands while pressing both palms together as people do when they pray, and breathe on the paper. You have made a binary talisman to protect your computer files.

Devoke.

Put the binary talisman somewhere hidden around your computer. Underneath it works well so that its protective energy can seep up into the machinery.

Magickal Wisdom: A spell can be broken.

If you cast a spell and regret it later, you can stop it by releasing its energy. Unlike a computer, which has a delete button, spells don't have an instant way to stop the change you set in motion. As you've already learned, doubting the spell after you cast it will make it less effective. But if you truly regret what you've done, if you realize it was unethical or that you don't want those results at all, the best course of action is to release the spell officially. Do this by going back into your circle and releasing the energy from the old spell. Rip the paper, break the wax, cut the cords, or untie the knots. Do it ritually with intention to reverse the spell. It's also good to add your voice to break the spell by saying something simple such as "I release the energy that bound this spell" or "What once was done is now released." If you can say and do it the opposite way that you cast the spell, so much the better. Finally, take the pieces and put them in salt, store them in the freezer overnight, to negate their charge, or bury them, burn them, or throw them in water to ground the energy. You're returning the parts to the earth to release the energy or at least you're neutralizing the energy the item had been holding so you can keep the item but rid it of that magickal purpose.

Spell 24: For Keeping One's Locker from Being Opened

YOU WILL NEED:
just yourself

As you prepare to do this spell, think about your locker as your private space and about how you're the only one who should open it while it's yours. There're hundreds of lockers that all look the same. Yours is special to you because it's where you keep your belongings. But to anyone else, it's just one in a long row, and you'll make this work to your advantage by asking the spirit of the locker to blend in with all the others.

I recommend that you start this process of preparing and thinking about this spell at home, but you'll actually cast this spell while at school in front of your locker. That's a big deal because it's probably your first spell where you'll be somewhere other than in your room with your altar. You'll go through the process of creating sacred space and casting the spell without your tools. Don't worry; you can do it.

The Spell: Meditate to ground and center while standing quietly in front of your locker. Stay standing in place to cast the circle by visualizing the ring of energy around you and your locker. Then call the quarters without speaking aloud by visualizing an eagle for east, a salamander for south, a dolphin for west, and a bear for north. It shouldn't take long to go through this process: only a minute or less.

You might have more of an adjustment to make in shifting consciousness, but your magick will work even if you're not in front of your altar without any tools in hand.

Stay standing straight in front of the locker when you're between the worlds. Take a deep breath and exhale it by forcing your breath out onto the locker. Visualize your breath going into the crack around the door as if it were caulk sealing it closed.

Say the following once, "Sticky shut, closed shut, keeping shut, staying shut until I return." You can speak this aloud or you can whisper it or you can mouth the words without saying anything. Use your judgment based on your surroundings. You don't want to have people come up to you and interrupt your spell, so try to be inconspicuous as you do this.

As imperceptibly as possible use your hands to make the motions of tying a knot in the air in front of the locker's handle. Pull the invisible knot tight. The knot is real, even though it's not visible in the physical world. Thank the quarters, and go away knowing that the locker is sealed until you return.

When you next return to your locker, clap or make some sort of loud snapping noise to release the spell. It also works to make the noise you're using by pretending you accidentally banged your locker door. The sound breaks the web of energy that's keeping the seal in place. Visualize the energy of the spell and the circle going down into the ground. Once the knot is undone and the seal is broken, you must start over to put the knot in place again. While I recommend that you don't repeat most spells often or cast more than one a day, you can use this one each time you go to your locker.

Magickal Wisdom: Believe; do not doubt.

Trust that your magick will work or you'll undermine its power to do so. This is such a simple lesson, yet it's hard to follow. Everyone who casts spells has had at least a fleeting thought, "I wonder if it worked?" Pow. That was a puncture in the magick right there. Don't look back. Doubt will kill the potency of any spell. Don't second-guess yourself. Looking for proof will also get you in trouble. Just try to prove magick, and you're in trouble. Other people may not believe that your magick worked, but you're not doing magick to prove anything to anyone else, are you? You just have to know for sure that your magick is effective and that the spell worked or for sure it will not work. It is better to forget that you did the spell in the first place than to question whether it will work.

Spell 25: Against Detention

YOU WILL NEED:
   your athame
   balloon
   tablespoon of flour
   pin
   small funnel
   (Note that this spell makes a small mess.)

In preparation concentrate on what happens in a detention. You're confined, and you may be given a task to do.

If you are given the detention because you didn't finish your homework, you may be told to work on your studies. If you are given the detention because you were caught doing something against the rules, you'll probably be forced to do something unpleasant such as cleaning at your school or staying in detention. Focus on how you feel when you're in detention. Do you feel like doing homework or cleaning up? I doubt it. The thought to put out to the universe is that if this is a sign to you, it's not an effective one. You can counter this by asking the universe's web of energy to find a better, more effective way to channel your energy.

Any flour will do, and you don't need more than a tablespoon of it. Any pin will do, even a safety pin. Be intentional. Keep your purpose firmly in mind as you search without being overly picky about the items you're collecting. The balloon, however, will take a bit of thought as far as the color goes. Choose a color that represents negativity to you. You could choose black to represent punishment. You could choose dark blue to represent the depression you feel when you get a detention. Or you could choose red to represent anger, yours, the teacher's, and perhaps even your parents'.

The Spell: Ground and center. Cast the circle.

When you're between the worlds, stand tall and concentrate on how much you hate detentions and how they're not productive for getting your work done or for changing your "bad behavior." Take your athame and hold it so that the tip of the point touches the balloon (not yet inflated). Say, "Detentions are unproductive, negative forces in my life, and I concentrate their negative energy and affects here in this balloon."

Next, take some of the flour and put it into the still-deflated balloon. Insert a small funnel into the balloon's neck. Then pour the flour into the still-deflated balloon as you say, "Negative situations can balloon out of proportion. They can seem worse than they are." To reduce mess, make sure you only use a little bit of flour. Then blow up the balloon being careful not to inhale the flour. Try breathing out only through your mouth and in through your nose. When you're done, knot the end closed in the normal way.

Raise the balloon directly overhead with your nondominant hand, and hold the pin ready to stab it in your other hand. Say, "I burst the negative energy of detentions to go away from me to elsewhere in the world." Stab the balloon so that it pops, preferably with a loud noise. Let the flour fall onto you as you absorb the positive energy back into your body now that the negativity is gone.

Devoke, and end by snapping your fingers to clear the excess energy to show that it's a snap to get rid of that negative energy. If you used a lot of flour, you may need to vacuum up the mess.

Magickal Wisdom: Destruction is a valid magickal force.

Most of the spells in this book involve white or good magick for positive results. Many people assume that black or destructure magick involves evil intent, but this isn't true. When used appropriately, destruction can be a positive direction for energy, but you must take great care to make sure that the destruction also follows the law "harm none." In this spell, you're popping the balloon to destroy it. With the balloon you're showing the universe how you want to diminish the negative energy of detentions in your life. Natural magick, like the natural world, includes both waxing and waning energy. Destruction and decay are part of the normal process in the cycle of life. Birth can't exist without death. Death isn't bad, but it can be scary. It's a major transition that will happen to all of us, and while alive, we don't know what it's like to die or to be dead.

But it's not up to each of us to kill another being without good reason. Killing in order to eat is okay. Whether you eat plants or animals, be thankful for what you need for your own sustenance. Don't waste. Without destruction and decay, our world would be too full, and so these forces keep our world in balance. When you need to use these forces, your destructive act of popping the balloon mirrors the diminishing you want the web of energy to do for you by taking away detentions from your life. Take great care whenever you cast a spell that involves destructive energy, for you'll assume the responsibility for what you destroyed.

Spell 26: For Eloquent Speaking

YOU WILL NEED:

paper

food coloring (preferably blue or green)

toothpick
mirror

It's easy to say something, but it's hard to make the words come out right when everyone is attentively listening to you. This spell is useful in many situations including if you're on a debating team or if you're giving an oral report.

As you prepare to do this work, think of the qualities you would like to have in order to be a good speaker. You want to speak clearly. You want to be understood. You want to be interesting. You want to make logical sense. And here you're giving a monologue. For the most part, you're not expecting a response other than maybe some brief questions, which you'll answer. So what we'll do in this spell is put a temporary tattoo on your tongue.

The paper you choose should be medium to thick. Don't choose tissue paper because it dissolves too easily when it gets wet, and this paper is going to get wet. Also, it's useful to have paper that is meant for writing because it's been prepared to take ink. Paper that hasn't had this treatment will allow any sort of ink to feather out rather than retain its shape.

Regular food coloring will do the trick. I suggest that you don't choose red, pink, yellow, or orange because they're too close to the pink color of your tongue. Blue is a great choice to emphasize communication because it corresponds with the fifth chakra, the energy center at your throat that rules communication in the body. Green is also good because it emphasizes luck.

The Spell: Ground and center. Cast the circle.

Sit down in the center of your circle. Face east, the direction in the circle that corresponds to Air and speaking. Take out your paper and breathe a puff of air onto it. Hold the paper between your palms with both hands closed and pressed together. Visualize yourself giving your report in front of the class or speaking in front of a group of people or whatever your situation is about to be. Include as many details as you can. If you know what the room looks like, then picture yourself in that room. If you know how large your audience will be, then picture yourself facing that group of people but looking up and beyond them to the back wall.

Then take out the food coloring and the toothpick. Put the toothpick in the food coloring so that the tip has enough liquid on it to use as a pen. Make this symbol on the piece of paper: ☿. This is the symbol for Mercury, the planet that corresponds to communication. Then sprinkle some nutmeg on it.

Pick up the paper and press the side you did not write on to the middle of your throat, and say, "Communication of Mercury come to me." Then take the paper and put the writing side down onto your tongue. Keep your mouth open, and do not chew. Leave the paper on your tongue for ten seconds. Taste the nutmeg and think about how it heightens your tongue's sensitivity to taste just the way you are increasing your tongue's ability to speak well in front of an audience. Then remove the paper and look at your tongue in the mirror. You should have a tattoo on your tongue. It will dissolve into your body, and as it does, you will absorb its potent communication power.

Devoke.

Practical note: Do not use pen ink or ink from a printer to do this. Food coloring is safe for consumption, and industrial inks are not.

Magickal Wisdom: The way you communicate the spell adds power to it.

Your spell will increase in effectiveness if what you say and do corresponds to the results you want from the spell. Rhyming, while not necessary, can make a spell powerful if it's a good, catchy rhyme because it's easy to repeat and remember. But rhyming isn't always easy, and it's more important to have a straight, nonrhyming, accurate statement than doggerel any day. A spell should not be a tongue twister or else you will need to concentrate too hard on how to say it rather than on the force behind it, the meaning that you're sending off. Alliteration can add power to a spell particularly if the letter that starts each word has a magickal connection to a rune (a magickal letter) in the spell you're doing. A spell doesn't need to have a spoken portion. It's possible that quiet or silence adds to the spell's power and that meditation or physical action is all that's needed. Before you cast any spell, give careful preparation to the way that you're communicating your request to the spirit world.

Spell 27: For Tests and Exams in Classes

YOU WILL NEED:

photocopies of some of the pages from the book you
are being tested on
scissors
glue
needle and black thread
nail file or emery board
yellow candle
matches
bell

As you prepare for this spell, keep your mind open to overachieving on this test or series of tests. Even if you get nervous to the point that it often affects your score or if you did not finish all the reading or studying that you had intended to do, you have the power to give correct answers. Think about taking the subject matter and going one step further with it to respond on the test in a way which shows the teacher you know the material beyond memorizing facts and that you have been thinking about the greater implications after analyzing the facts. Concentrate on staying calm and keeping the information readily accessible in your mind.

Make random photocopies of various pages in your textbook. You do not need more than three pages.

It's important to use your time wisely when studying for a test. You have to concentrate mainly on studying. But you'll also need to take some breaks in order to study efficiently. If you feel pressed for time before a test, you can cast this spell during a study break. The exact amount of time it takes to cast a spell varies, but by keeping spells such as this one brief, say no more than fifteen minutes, then you're concentrating your energy effectively. Taking longer to cast a spell isn't bad, but it's easier to lose your focus.

The Spell: Ground and center. Cast the circle.

When you're between the worlds, sit down and light your yellow candle. Students are famous for studying late by candlelight, so you will cast this spell with the candle burning on your altar. Yellow is the color associated with learning and knowledge, so as you light it say, "Candle burn bright to enlighten my mind with the knowledge I need to know for this test."

Then cut out four rectangles about 3 inches high and 5 inches wide from the photocopies you made of the reading you'll be tested on. It doesn't matter if the subject is English, math, or co-ed naked soccer as long as the textbook photocopies are the same subject as the test. (If you're making this for exams, then make photocopies from each of the subjects. This won't be quite as focused as if you create the talisman for one subject, but it's still possible to do the spell this way.) Then fold each section in half so that the 5-inch sides are now halved by the fold like a book but the paper is still 3 inches high. Stack the four folded sections inside one another so that they become pages. Then use the needle and black thread to sew the folded parts as if you're binding a book. No need to be a perfectionist here. You're just making a couple of quick stitches. Your intent is much more important than the quality of your sewing. You're binding a book, but this will become a talisman. Keep your focus on binding the knowledge you need into the book and your ability to test well.

Next, open the middle page of the book, and flatten it out. Put some glue on the pages (not too much or it will wrinkle). Then take out your nail file or emery board and use it to file down the nails on your dominant hand so that you create some particles. Sprinkle this nail dust onto the glue. Then shut the two middle pages together so that they're glued shut. Finish by gluing all the pages together so that you cannot access the information inside the book. As you glue the last page down, say, "The book is shut, the matter is sealed. I will find I tested well when the results are revealed."

Carry this talisman with you when you take your test. If a teacher or anyone sees this book you made, show them that you glued it completely shut, and say that you made it for good luck.

Devoke. Try ringing the bell to ground the energy and clear the space.

Magickal Wisdom: Once an item is charged, preserve your intention with that item.

Use an item that was charged in a spell for only one magickal purpose. Don't mix spells up. If you charge an item, such as the book talisman in this spell, that is one purpose, and you shouldn't use that same item you made for a different spell later. You may wonder why you can use your tools from one spell to the next but not something from a spell. You've charged the tools for the purpose of help while doing magick, so that is consistent with their original purpose. If you light a candle for one purpose and blow it out before it's burned down (we all need to leave the room sometimes), then don't light it again during another spell. You can light it later to finish releasing the energy in that original spell, but you shouldn't change the results you want or else your message will be garbled. You can use a general altar candle each time you sit at your altar, but not a candle charged with energy for a particular purpose other than illuminating your altar. The same is true of this book talisman that you've made. Use it for this test or series of exams, but it should be specific to the subject and not for too long a period, say no more than a week or two. When the test or exams are over, release its energy and make another if you need one again.

Spell 28: For Help Taking SATs and Other Standardized Tests

YOU WILL NEED:
   7 ice cubes
   small bowl

As you prepare for this spell, think clearly about the important but not overly important role of standardized tests. Picture yourself reading the test booklet and knowing exactly what to do. Visualize the answers flowing like water from your hand as you fill out your answer sheet.

Choose seven relatively large ice cubes. Also choose a small bowl to put them in. (The spell will be more effective if you make the ice cubes yourself, but it is not necessary.)

The Spell: Ground and center. Cast the circle.

Between the worlds, squat with your hands on the ground, then stand with your hands up to the sky, and then put your hands back on the ground. As you do this, visualize bringing energy up from the earth into yourself, then down from the sky, then again up from the earth.

Next, put each ice cube in the bowl while keeping in mind the standardized test you will soon take. Say, "With the power of energy to melt ice and change it to liquid, I call forth water to loosen the flow of information within me and guide my hands to the right answers. If I freeze up, my inner power will melt that ice." Put the bowl of ice on your altar and wait for the ice to melt. Or if you want the melting to happen faster, put it near a heater or in a sunny spot. When all the ice melts, rub some of the water on the back of your hands and on your palms.

Devoke.

Magickal Wisdom: Get the timing right.

Don't do a spell for an outcome when the outcome is already decided. It may seem obvious that you can't change your grade once it's already been given, but I point it out because you may have more time than you think in order to do this spell. The most powerful time to do it is before you take the test because the spell has the longest time to get your desired results. But you can also do the spell after taking the test. Your spell won't influence your performance during the test, but there's still time for the influence to affect your score. It's okay to do a spell for positive test results before you know what the results are, such as when your score is still in the mail. But once you know the results, don't do the spell because you can't change the results. If your timing is good, your spell will have increased potency.

Spell 29: For Support from a Teacher

YOU WILL NEED:
   two green ribbons (2 to 3 feet long)
   dried sage
   matches
   nonflammable surface to catch ash.

Teachers have a lot of control in your life, and it is often not apparent that what they do on your behalf really is in your best interest. Nevertheless, there are times when you would benefit from having a teacher on your side. A good teacher will look for the best in you and support you. So, concentrate on how to gain an ally from this type of authority when you need it most.

As you prepare for this spell, concentrate on the situation that you're in. Maybe you've been caught not turning in your homework again. Or maybe you need to ask a teacher to write you a recommendation. You're asking for support when you need it but don't know what would help you the most. You're not asking for someone else, such as a teacher, friend, or parent to remove the tension, you're asking for support so that you've a productive way to solve this problem.

You'll use green ribbons because green is the color of great strength and growth. Think of a blade of grass that grows in the cement sidewalk. It may not seem mightier than a sword, but it can cut through cement. With this spell, you too will find the strength to find your way out of a difficult situation. The ribbon should be anywhere from ¼ inch wide to 3 inches wide. A width between ½ to 1 inch will be the easiest to use. Make sure that the ribbon is at least 2 feet, preferably 3 feet long.

The Spell: Ground and center. Cast the circle.

Once you're in sacred space between the worlds, visualize that blade of grass that pushes its way up to grow through the cracks in cement and rocks. Say, "By the power of the ancient blade that wields strength in the natural world, I call for support."

Light the sage and burn some until it smokes. Blow on the sage to increase the smoke and wave the ribbons on both sides through the smoke to purify and consecrate them for this purpose.

Next wrap one ribbon around your ankle starting with the dominant side (if you're right-handed, wrap your right ankle). Leave about 4 to 6 inches hanging loose from where you start. As you wrap the ribbon, try to overlap the previous layer of ribbon just a little bit and extend the rest of the ribbon over a different part of your ankle so that your entire ankle is covered as if you were putting on an ace bandage. The ribbon should be snug so that it stays where you lay it down but not too tight because you don't want it to cut off your circulation. When you have only a little bit of ribbon left, tie it off with the piece you left loose at the beginning. It doesn't matter what kind of knot you use as long as it stays tight so the ribbon doesn't fall off. As you do this, think about how ankles support your whole body by connecting your feet to the rest of you. Then repeat this process with the ankle on your nondominant side (if you're right-handed, wrap your left ankle).

When you're finished wrapping both ankles, say, "Those with authority do not have power over me, they have the power to help me. I call on the mentor's dedication to help students grow so that I can gain support." Do not use a specific person's name. You want to leave this open so that help can come, not only from where you expect it, but from where you least expect it as well. If you name a specific person, you're trying to force them to help. But if you're not naming someone specific, you're asking whoever is right for this situation to recognize it and step forward which benefits you because it gives you more options.

Devoke, and end by making three small jumps with both feet in order to ground the energy.

Wear the wraps for at least fifteen minutes and preferably longer.

Magickal Wisdom: Manipulative magick is bad even if your intention is good.

Do not try to have power over someone else or to force someone to do something. Many people turn to magick initially thinking they will gain control over other people, get a slave, force someone to do one's bidding, or coerce someone to fall in love. These are all corrupt uses of power that do not lead to the path of spiritual purity and development. And they are not necessary. You can use other, better ways of winning friends and influencing people without going into debt with your karma, which is an Eastern concept that translates to mean a spiritual bank account. The spiritual world does not recognize or respond to authority in the same way that the physical world does. Power over someone else is a physical concept no matter how it is manifested. The spiritual web of energy recognizes each person, animal, plant, and object because of distinct character traits and energy, not according to how rich, good-looking, or charismatic the individual is.

A common misuse of magick is to pray or cast spells for people without asking consent beforehand. Even if you have the good intention of sending healing energy to someone sick without wanting to bother the person beforehand, this is manipulative magick. You cannot know what is in someone else's best interest. Always ask for consent before casting a spell that would affect someone else.

Spell 30: For Aid from a Student

YOU WILL NEED:

jellybeans of various colors
small box with lid

When you're in a bind, you might want a friend, new or old, to help you. Think about the unspoken bond that students have with each other in the face of a common adversary.

While you find the jellybeans you'll need, think of how you lend a hand to a friend in need. If your friend needs help, part of your job as a good friend is to help out. Even if you have to go out of your way a little bit, your friend is worth it. And if you don't have to go out of your way, you'd probably help someone you don't know yet. That's an act of charity that could even start a friendship. And in thinking about how you'd lend a hand, think about how there are times when you could use an extra hand. Part of being a friend is allowing friends to give help and accepting it gracefully.

The Spell: Ground and center. Cast the circle.

When you are between the worlds, stand tall and take a deep breath. As you do, visualize a glowing, green light around your heart. Green is the color associated with healing and with the heart chakra. Feel its warmth and notice how your heart seems to expand when you concentrate on it. Pick up your jellybeans and hold them in your hand with your fingers closed over them. Press your closed fist to your heart and meld your hand and the jellybeans into the energy you have built around your heart.

Say, "Let the power of bonding encourage friendship in my life. When I see a friend in need, an old friend or a person who may become a new friend, I help out. And when I need help, an old friend or a person who will become a new friend will help me."

Take two green jellybeans. Chew one edge of each down the length of the jellybean. Lick the chewed edges and hold them together until they stick. Your saliva will break down the sugars in the jellybeans just enough so that the two stay together. When they're stuck together, say, "Bond of friendship!"

Do the same with two pink jellybeans, but this time say, "Code of peers!"

Next, breathe on your small box, and put the two pairs of jellybeans in the box and seal it closed (no need for bugs or rodents to get to it). Now hold the box, and say, "Bond of friendship, code of peers, help me cut my trouble like shears."

Devoke.

Wait at least fifteen minutes before opening the box. Preferably wait overnight and let the moonlight fall onto the box (take it outside or put it on a windowsill).

Magickal Wisdom: Accept responsibility for your magick.

By casting spells, you're making changes in the world, changes that you personally caused. That means that you're responsible for what happens. In many cases, nothing bad will happen. If you're having trouble with math and you cast a spell to ask a student to help you study, a fellow student may ask you to study together so that you both know the subject better. That's good for both of you. But it doesn't always work like that. If you demand that a friend come to your aid, you may be asking someone you like to be with you when the friend should be off doing something else. Or if you start considering shortcut options, such as how to cheat on the test rather than study for it, you might both get in trouble. And then you're responsible for your friend because you're the one who called the friend to the situation in the first place. Before casting any spell, ask yourself if you're willing to take responsibility for the result.

Adeptitude

Another meditation, another way to cast the circle, and many more spells have brought you to the end of your days as an apprentice. You are now able to protect yourself from difficult homework, class snoozing, and detentions. You can guard your computer files, heighten your abilities to take tests, and call someone to help when you need it.

As spells work, you have no doubt recognized that you are one small part of an infinite whole. Yet despite how great the web of the world around you is, you have the ability to change your environment with magick. Because everything in that web is interconnected, when you make one tug, you set the universe in motion to bring what you need to you. And it is not hard if you are using your most important tool correctly. What is that tool? It is your own body because it harnesses your energy and psychic power. You already had this knowledge within you, and you proved it to yourself as you cast your first spell away from your altar.

What is your most important tool?

You. **You are your most important tool.**

You have made your way through half of the spells in this book. So from here on out, the spells will increase in intensity. Where before you could cast one a day, I recommend that you space the upcoming spells at least three days apart. If you're wise, you'll leave even more time than that between spells. In the next chapter, "The Sorcerer: Spells About Fun, Sports, and Hobbies," you will discover the answer to the question: How can you make your spells gain in intensity? Proceed and meet the sorcerer within you.

CHAPTER 4

THE SORCERER: SPELLS ABOUT FUN, SPORTS, AND HOBBIES

YOU'VE BEEN CASTING SPELLS for a while now, and you've probably noticed that they work. Maybe that was even surprising to you. It shouldn't be. You have power within you, and you're just channeling it in a focused way with ordinary actions to make changes in yourself and your environment. By casting spells, you are just using a different method of channeling your energy. Or if you're doing both ordinary actions and spells combined, which is the best way, you're enhancing, increasing, and quickening the changes you want. You're making changes that are more complete.

This chapter gives you eight spells relating to the fun part of your life, extracurricular activities such as sports, drama, and art. You may not be interested in all these areas, but try to do at least three of them. There's probably some reason you'll need to increase your focus in a sport or hobby, and sometimes you'll play a game that needs scoring and winning. There are spells for the artistic types and for those who are babysitting. Some of these spells are more difficult than the ones in the preceding chapter because these spells involve situations in which you're interacting with people. It's one thing to have people nearby and a completely different thing to have to consider interacting with them while casting spells. That may not seem like a big deal at first, but it complicates the ethical issues surrounding magick. If you're not paying attention, you could rack up some unpleasant karma. I recommend avoiding that.

It's just about this time that most people will slack off writing in the book of shadows. Did I catch you? Do you even remember where you put it? You'll have an easier time with the magickal world if you keep up your magickal book of shadows. It's an important tool over time, but it's not obvious that this is the case until some time has passed. At which point it's too late. Even if you're slogging through it, keep going. I promise you it's worth it. You'll be able to look up details about the spells you cast so that you can use them as springboards for new magickal work.

Here is your grounding and centering meditation for the spells in this chapter. In this meditation, you liken your body to the process of a seed sprouting and growing into a plant. It's a powerful metaphor that will help you be fully in your body to work magick. It's more advanced than the previous grounding and centering meditations because it's not just about becoming aware of your body but of knowing each part of your body as it moves. It's one thing to meditate while staying still and another while moving.

Grounding and Centering Meditation: The Plant Growing

Crouch on the ground in a squatting position. Take a deep breath and hold it for a couple of seconds.

Then exhale and slowly begin to unroll and go up. Push up through your feet, and feel the energy rise up through your legs. Feel the roundness of your back. Unfold your arms and straighten them as you become more upright. Finally, feel the top of your spine align with your neck and put your head above it as you come to a full standing position. Feel the crown of your head above you and your feet firmly below you at the same time.

Take another deep breath, and staying still, exhale again. When you are solidly grounded, you have prepared yourself fully.

Here is how to cast the circle for the spells in this chapter. In this manner of casting the circle and calling quarters, you will use classic earth magick by invoking the power of the growth cycle.

Circle Casting: The Seasons

Stand at the edge of the circle in the north. Hold your athame pointing in front of you and stride to the east in order to join the north to the east. Take long, strong steps as you go. Be deliberate each time you pick up a foot and put one down. Then continue striding from east to south. Again, stride as you go from south to west and finish, striding as you go from west to north so that you have made a circle.

Make this circle with deliberate strides two more times for a total of three. By the time you're done, you should feel a solid ring of energy that you created with your steps while holding your athame.

Put your athame down and pick up your wand. Stand holding your wand in the north.

Turn to the east, and say, "In spring the world becomes warm and plants sprout."

Turn to the south, and say, "In summer the world becomes hot and plants grow."

Turn to the west, and say, "In fall the world becomes cool and plants ripen."

Turn to the north, and say, "In winter the world becomes cold and plants wither."

Stand in the Center and say, "The seasons revolve in a cycle. Each year brings new growth to replace the previous year's plants. The circle contains all parts of this cycle and stands to protect the regeneration of new life from old. The circle is cast."

The Spells

Spell 31: For Focus

YOU WILL NEED:

pebble

piece of paper

pen

small string

No matter what you're doing, you'll do better if you're able to focus well. As you get ready to do this spell, think of how your concentration and focus help you no matter what you're doing from reading to sports to casting spells. Think of how concentration makes a difficult task possible, even easy.

Your pebble should be relatively small, no bigger than $1/4$ inch in diameter. You'll know if it's the right pebble by noticing if it feels just right in your palm. That may sound odd, but you'll know it when you feel it.

You need a piece of paper cut into a circle at least 4 inches in diameter.

The Spell: Ground and center. Cast the circle.

When you're between the worlds, draw on your paper so that you make a bull's-eye on it. Make between three and five concentric circles, and color in the middle one so that it is dark. If your circle were a dartboard, hitting that dark center would be worth the most points.

Now take your pebble. Hold it a foot from your face. Look at it clearly and then look at something far beyond it. Bring it slowly toward your face while holding your eyes' focus on the item across the room. When it's about a few inches from your face, you will seem to see two pebbles and be able to see through them. Think about that. How can you see double and at the same time see through something? When you bring the pebble all the way to your forehead between your eyes, you won't see it at all. This is your blind spot. Very few items have ever been in your blind spot because you are naturally protective of this place since you cannot see it. You have charged this pebble magickally now because you have allowed it to be in your blind spot at your third eye. Your third eye is the spot in the middle of the forehead that is a center for "seeing" spiritually. It's also the sixth chakra, the energy center that corresponds to spiritual thinking.

Take the pebble and put it in the middle of the bull's-eye you created. Crush some rosemary in your hands and sprinkle it over the pebble. As you do this, concentrate on how the rosemary corresponds to seeing and how focus requires steady sight. Fold the paper up around the pebble, twist the paper closed, and tie the string around the paper just above the pebble to keep the pebble on the bull's-eye. As you do this, say, "From my third eye to this bull's-eye, I put this magickal pebble so that my focus will stay strong and steady."

Devoke.

Magickal Wisdom: Keep your magickal focus.

Keep your focus and concentrate on where you're directing energy and for what purpose. Keeping your focus means intensifying your magick. It's important what you do with your mind during the spell. Distractions will dissipate the flow of energy you're producing. Therefore, a simple spell with solid, focused psychic power is more effective than a long, involved spell during which your focus wanders a couple of times. The focus spell is another example showing that what's true in the ordinary world is also true in the magickal world. Here you're asking for focus for a mundane activity because you know that if you're not paying attention the other team will score while you're daydreaming or you'll miss an important opportunity. The same is true of magickal work, so opt for short constant focus rather than long unsustainable focus.

Spell 32: For Impenetrable Defense

YOU WILL NEED:

    plastic bag that seals by squeezing a strip together
    small piece of blank paper
    pen
    incense
    bowl of water
    ten or more small stones or pebbles

As you prepare for this spell, think of a strong defense in its many forms. A castle built on a tall cliff is a stronghold for its people. A vault in a bank is a stronghold for money. And your defense is a stronghold against the opponent's attempts to score.

The Spell: Ground and center. Cast the circle.

When you're between the worlds, stand tall, and say, "My defensive force is strong. The goal I protect is impenetrable."

Draw a picture of your goal or defensive area on the paper. You can draw yourself into the picture, but don't add any other people. Don't worry about your drawing ability. The straight lines of markings on a playing field or court will work fine. Put the piece of paper inside the plastic bag. Then scrape under your fingernails and put any stuff you get from under them into the bag with the goal. Putting a physical part of yourself increases the spell's connection to you. As you seal it, say, "I envelope my vulnerable goal with this protective shield." Hold it above your head and then press it down on the floor. Make sure it's sealed tightly.

With the bag as a shield for this symbolic goal, you're going to expose it to the elements. Start by lighting some incense and wafting the smoke over the bag as you hold it. Then put the bag on the floor and drop the small stones or pebbles on it. Next, swish the plastic bag in the bowl of water. Each time you do, say, "Shield be strong, a score is wrong. Shield stay tight, a shutout is right."

Say, "My impenetrable defense is set. Nothing can break the protective shield covering it. So be it!"

Devoke, and end by jumping three times letting your feet land together with a thud.

Leave the goal in the bag until at least after your game.

Note that if you have something other than a goal to defend or protect, you can draw a different picture and do this spell effectively. If you want to protect yourself, for example, you could use a photo of yourself.

Magickal Wisdom: Focus your spells in the positive.

You'll notice that all the spells in this book are either "for" or "against" something. And if you look closely, all the against spells turn out to be for the opposite of what they're against. For example, previously you had a spell against a pimple, but if you look closely, the spell's focus was for making the pimple diminish. That's because the magickal world doesn't understand negativity the way we do. Both "I want a new dog" and "I don't want a new dog" will yield the same results: a new dog. Cast your spells "for something" rather than asking "not for something." If you're looking for something to go away, don't say "Not this" say "Avoid this," and you'll have a much better chance of the magick occurring. This spell could've been "to not let the other team score," and after you focused on that, the other team would've scored a lot because the spirit world would honor the motion (scoring) and the target (the other team). Negatives are a human refinement of language. By asking "for strong defense," you're sending the message so that the magickal world will respond with the results you want.

Spell 33: For Winning

YOU WILL NEED:
> strip of thick card stock
> some leaves
> exacto knife or hole punch
> invisible tape

As you prepare for this spell, think of the feeling you get when you win something you really worked hard at and wanted to win. Envision your strong performance that leads to winning, and imagine the feeling you get when you play at your best ability.

The strip of paper should be a thick card stock and between ½ inch and 2 inches wide. Cut the length so that it fits around your head and has a slight overlap. (This spell can also be done with flexible metal wire that you bend around your head, but you'll have to get the wire and wire cutters, so paper may be convenient to use.)

Go outside and find some leaves. Generally, I'd suggest laurel leaves because these are symbolic of victory, but any leaves that look majestic and regal to you will do. You're going to create a victory crown. It's best to find leaves that have already fallen off the trees, but it's okay if you take a leaf off a living tree if you ask and receive permission. Taking a few leaves isn't going to kill a tree. (In fact, often pruning a tree makes it grow better.) If it's spring or summer, you'll find luscious green leaves. In fall, you'll probably have flaming yellow, orange, and red leaves available in abundance. In winter you can get fake leaves at a craft store, or better yet, use some evergreen trimmings.

The Spell: Ground and center. Cast the circle.

Hold the leaves you gathered, and say, "Leaves, thank you for joining me in my spell." Lay them down in front of you delicately, looking at each one and admiring it as you do.

Take a deep breath, and hold your strip of paper. Make holes in the paper by slicing slits in it with the exacto knife or creating holes with the hole punch and then weave the leaves through the holes or attach the leaves with tape. Try to get the leaves so they're pointing up with the stems down or hidden on the backside of the paper. The backside is also a good place for reinforcing tape to hold the leaves in place. Think about how you're going to put the crown on once you've made it. The leaves need to stay attached and pointing upwards. If you have to adjust it, that's okay, but it's best if it's secure beforehand and doesn't need adjusting.

When you finish creating the crown, hold it with both hands over your head, and say, "Individually you are leaves, but together you make a victory crown. I place you on my head so that glorious victory will come to me." Place the crown on your head as if you were crowning yourself. Soak in that feeling of winning and being king or queen of your sport while wearing this crown.

As you wear the crown, say, "Victory comes to me." Start by making a statement as if you were saying it once. Then repeat it. Continue saying it again and again building up the speed, tone, and intensity of the statement. When you reach a peak of speed, high tone, and intensity, imagine shooting off the energy of the chant into the sky as if it were a shooting star. When you are done, take off the crown and devoke. Stomp on the floor to ground the energy.

Gently and lovingly take apart the crown and put all the natural materials outside by a tree. Nobody else should ever wear this crown.

Magickal Wisdom: Together your thoughts and feelings magnify a spell's power.

Combining thoughts and feelings gives your psychic energy more power. You may notice that as you read the spells in this book you first go through a thought process to prepare for the spell. Then during the spell, you often add an emotional feeling. When you combine your thoughts and feelings while doing magickal work, you're mixing as much of your personal power as you can. The more you add to a spell this way, the more effective it will be. You're using your full force, mind, body, and soul, to cast the spell, and you're directing the energy and sending it off with your psychic power. And when you do this, the sum of the parts is more than the individual parts added together. The power increases geometrically. Thoughts and feelings aren't "one plus one equals two;" they magnify in power to equal three.

Spell 34: For Getting a Good Part in the Play

YOU WILL NEED:
   stiff piece of paper
   scissors or an exacto knife
   hole punch
   pen
   string at least 18 inches long

As you prepare for this spell, try not to focus on a particular part you want to play. Find out what play the director has chosen, and do what you can to prepare for the auditions. But remember that you needn't have the lead role to steal the show. You could be on the stage the shortest amount of time and be the best actor in the production. A stellar performance will lead to being cast again in bigger and better roles, and setting your sights high will help you attain your goals in the long run. For now, however, what's going to help you the most is to be cast in the part that shows off your skill and talent the most so that you'll be noticed and remembered in a positive way.

In order to play a part well, you need to become that other character on stage. Think about this temporary transformation. How does an actor embody another person's walk, manner of speech, gestures, and personality? But remember to leave the spell open so that the web of magick can lead you in the direction that will help you even more than the direction you think is best. You may want the lead role, but if you end up with another part, it may be the universe's way of giving you the part that shows off your talent better and that leads a local scout to recruit you to theater beyond your school.

You're going to mimic having a role in a play by wearing a mask. If you feel that a costume would be a better fit for you during this spell, it's fine to do that along with the mask or instead of it. But remember that you don't want to be too specific about what character you are while wearing the costume. You could attempt to dress in something generic to the time period of the play you'll audition for, such as a Roman toga or Shakespearean dress. Or you could try to wear something that's archetypal of theater in general, such as the comedy or tragedy masks.

The Spell: Ground and center. Cast the circle.

Begin by making a mask. Cut the paper into an oval shape that will cover your face. Draw a face on the mask.

The eyes generally go halfway between the top and bottom of the oval. Cut out the space for the eyes. You can cut a nose hole, but it's not absolutely necessary. The mouth hole is more important because you'll be speaking during this spell. Punch a hole about $\frac{1}{2}$ inch from the edge on either side of oval where ears would be. Cut the string in half, and pull it through the holes, attaching each piece to the mask. Purposefully leave the mask free of decoration. You want it to be mostly blank so that it could be the face of any character in any play. Even though you're not making a specific character, you're doing magick in creating a generic face. Be conscious of creating this mask as a magickal act.

When you finish the mask, take a deep, cleansing breath and put it (or your costume) on. Stand in the center of the circle, and say, "I want to act. I want to perform on the stage. See the transformation I have started here, and complete it by giving me the role that will make my talent shine." Put out your arms and spin fast in a circle. When you're dizzy, say "It is so!" and lie down on the floor. As you lie there recovering, your mind will spin and it's a good time to receive information from your subconscious perhaps about what you may need to do to help this spell with your follow-up, mundane actions. Maybe you will have an image pop into your head about what's the best part to try out for or what to do during your audition. That's how it works for me, but be open to finding out how it will work for you.

Devoke.

Magickal Wisdom: The universe is out to help you.

Leave room in your spell to get help from the web of magick. Being too specific about what you want and how you want to get it doesn't give room for the universe to respond by nudging you beneficially. If you leave room in your spells for spiritual guidance, you will get results that are even better for you than what you asked for. Leave it up to the web of energy in the spirit world to bring you something better than you think you want or need. That's why this spell specifically tells you not to think of the part in the play that you want.

Spell 35: For Having an Easy Time While Babysitting

YOU WILL NEED:

    a small bowl of water

    a (blue, orange, or white) candle

    matches

While you're babysitting, you'll want to have an easy time of it. As you prepare for this spell, think of what makes an easy time while taking care of a baby or kids. A calm, happy baby is easy to take care of. Kids who play with each other or who you can easily entertain also make babysitting go by quickly. The key here is the emotions. You don't want the baby or kids to focus on the sadness or anger of missing their parents. You want them to be happy to spend time with you. Here's the hard part of this spell: you can't think about those specific children or else you'd be including them in your magick and that would influence them. Try instead to focus on yourself while working.

Find a small bowl. It must be big enough to hold water and have the candle in it. Choose a light blue candle for friendship or an orange candle for cooperation. A white candle is fine for peace.

The Spell: Ground and center. Cast the circle.

When you're between the worlds, stand in the center and hold your bowl of water. Exhale on it. Say, "Water, you who govern the emotions, I call to you now. While I babysit, bring gentle, calm waves of feeling my way."

Set the candle in the middle of the bowl and light it. Say, "For peace, for friendship, for cooperation while I'm working." Set the bowl on your altar so that the candle can burn down. Now laugh. Think of something funny and let laughter fill the circle.

Devoke, and end by clapping your hands three times.

Magickal Wisdom: What you send out comes back to you intensified.

The magick you do and energy you put out in the world comes back to you. Do you remember the saying "You catch more flies with sugar than with vinegar"? This saying means that if you're nice to others, you'll get more help and life will be easier. This is also true in the spiritual world. The more positive energy that you send out, the better off you'll be. On a mundane level, people will want to help you more. But it's also true in magick, the more good energy you send out, the more you'll receive in return, and it has a tendency to come back to you at just the right moment. You'll know it when something unexpected and good happens and you stop to say to yourself how great that was. The world will also be a better place. The other part of this lesson is that the magick magnifies by three before coming back to you. This is called "the threefold law," and it means that whatever you put out not only comes back to you but comes back with three times the force. So, if you cast a spell for someone to slip and fall on a banana peel, this spell would boomerang back to you so that you'd go flying off your bicycle and break a leg. You can see why it's a good idea to use positive magick.

Spell 36: For Creative Writing

YOU WILL NEED:

paper

scissors

pen or pencil

Writing is a basic way to express emotions and communicate. If you want to write stories, you'll want twisty plots and well-rounded characters. If you want to become a journalist, you'll want to get inside the heads of the key people and learn what led to the events you're reporting. If you're an emerging poet, you'll want to capture the essence of images in words. You can also use this spell to inspire a really good book of shadows for yourself.

As you prepare for this spell, think of all the times throughout the day that you write. You do your homework, you write in your magickal book of shadows, you jot down a telephone message, you write a note to pass in class, you sign up for a course. We take it for granted that everyone can write, but it used to be a special skill reserved for a class of scribes. As a writer, you join this elite group of people, so be conscious of every time you write something down. Writing allows you to communicate with people who aren't present, and that is special and powerful.

Choose the type of paper you want to write on. It can be fine paper or ordinary paper, but it's best to be a piece of loose paper rather than a part of a notebook or journal. Choose the type of writing implement that you find most comfortable.

Also, think about your goal. You'll want to have some sort of goal for your writing. Maybe you want a short story you've written to be published. Maybe you want to do well in a writing contest you'd like to enter. Perhaps you'd like to get an A on a creative writing assignment you're turning in. I suggest you avoid exorbitant goals such as becoming the most famous writer ever. That will take a long time to come true, and it's debatable what constitutes the most famous writer ever.

The Spell: Ground and center. Cast the circle.

Take your piece of paper and hold it in both hands. Feel the heat of your body collecting and building in your hands. Feel the warmth go from one hand to the other and back again with the paper in between.

Pick up your pen and hold it while saying "Muse, I call to you to fill me with inspiration. May the words I want to say flow through me onto paper. I ask you to guide me, to fill me with the words I need, and to stay with me as I write." Next, write your goal on the piece of paper.

Fold the paper in half three times and put it on your altar. Don't open it for at least nine days. When the spell has done its work, burn this piece of paper in a fireplace, barbecue, or grill. Any flame will do as long as you're careful to do the burning over a nonflammable surface (fire, after all, is dangerous). Fire is cleansing and purifying, and you're releasing the energy this way.

Devoke.

Magickal Wisdom: Be precise with your request.

Mean what you say, and say what you mean. Even if you're not using words, make your intention clear. When you're casting a spell, you're putting a lot of energy behind a request for change (not in how the change will happen, but the end results). You really want something to happen. You may have prepared in the mundane world beforehand. You'll probably follow-up after the spell with actions in the physical world. Given that your spell combines your mind, body, and spirit to make this request, imagine if you asked for the wrong thing. After putting the full force of your entire being into the spell, that wouldn't be so good, would it? As with creative writing, the words you choose matter. Careful attention to planning your spell's intention will pay off after your spell is cast. Be precise about what you want.

Spell 37: For Artistic Excellence

YOU WILL NEED:

   paper

   scissors

   glue

   regular pen or pencil

   colored pencils or markers

   pictures or found objects for a collage (choose
     anything that inspires you artistically)

Art is the most basic, perhaps even primal, way we have of expressing ourselves and capturing the essence of beauty and life around us. Whether you want to pursue a career in art later or just enjoy it as a pastime, you'll want to develop your own internal eye for color, form, and light. Concentrate on developing your unique sense of style to lead you to artistic excellence and, if you want it, recognition as well.

As you gather materials for this spell, try to think about how every person has the ability to be creative whether or not he or she uses the label "artist" as a self-description. As you choose your paper, markers, pencils, or glue, and decorative paper for the collage, pick up each one by itself, and ask it either aloud or silently if it wants to be part of this spell. If you get a "No," and you might, put it down and find another. Start first with the medium you like best. If you like watercolors, then find a set of paints. If you draw, find charcoal. If your favorite form of art is something that takes a long time or uses specialized equipment such as block printing or monotype, I suggest that you start simply at first and then add more detailed, sophisticated decorations later.

When you have gathered all your materials together, place them on the ground in front of your altar.

The Spell: Ground and center. Cast the circle.

Take a deep breath, and holding your wand with both hands, say, "Like the circle of life that goes on and on, like the path of the earth around the sun, I call forth my inner power to spiral forth and guide me as I create." Visualize white and yellow light coming up from the earth, down from the sky, and out from the natural world around you to your wand. Visualize that energy filling up your wand and going into your body and filling you up.

Next sit down and cut your paper into a circle with a diameter of at least 6 inches, preferably more. Draw two concentric circles inside the round paper dividing the paper into three sections equidistant from each other. Next, draw six equidistant spokes from the center of the circle out to the edge of the paper. (That is three lines across the diameter of the circle.) You have created a *mandala*. Mandala is the Sanskrit word meaning "circle," but it also connotes connection with community and the world. Although the mandala is a Buddhist concept, they parallel the circle that you cast before casting each spell. It's a universal symbol used for meditating.

Then turn over the circle so that it's face-down on the floor. Take out some peppercorns and put them on the face down paper. Use the palm of your hand to roll them around on the paper which will activate their power to connect your sense of touch to this spell so that you feel your artistic style within you.

In each of the sections in the innermost circle, write the words *light, dark, shape, space, color,* and *clearness*. In the middle sections put a representation of each of the primary colors bordered by the two secondary colors that mix with other primary colors to make those secondary colors (for example, the order: red, orange, yellow, green, blue, purple; not the order: red, blue, yellow, purple, orange, green). The outermost ring is for your personal symbols. You might choose to decorate each section with a different media that you like such as watercolor paints, magic markers, collage, or colored pencil. You might persue different techniques within a medium or places you want your art to appear (for example, on murals, on book covers, and in frames on walls). Figuring out how best to decorate this mandala for your goal is part of the spell. I can't tell you what to choose, but I can say that what you choose will help you in your artistic endeavors.

Stand holding your art mandala in front of your torso with the decoration facing out. Say, "I allow my subconscious to come forth and give expression through light and dark, shape and blank space, color and clearness, to guide me to my artistic excellence. So be it!"

Devoke, and end by clapping your hands.

Put your art mandala somewhere near where you create art (in your studio if you have one or by your desk if that's where you keep your supplies). Or you could put it near your bed to inspire your dreams.

Magickal Wisdom: Sleep on it.

This old advice about getting enough rest takes on a new meaning when applied to working magick. Not only do you regenerate while sleeping, but the world and especially you, mind, body, and spirit, both receive time to absorb the new direction of energy you have just sent out. I find this particularly true in any artistic pursuit. You could have a dream that points you in the right direction by showing you exactly what to do or by giving you a great idea for what to do. A dream is a fairly direct way of being inspired, but while you sleep, you can also have more subtle inspiration for art that also involves your spiritual growth.

Your subconscious may change your perspective on your art and guide you in a new way when you wake up without you realizing that this even happened. Oftentimes when I've been actively creating something artistic, I find that when I wake up after sleeping, I don't feel rested. But I'll also notice I have an idea of what to do with my art project. And I don't necessarily remember a dream about it. While you're asleep your body can work just as hard spiritually as while you're awake. It's a different kind of work, tiring because you feel extra groggy and not rested after sleep, but this tends to produce deep changes in your mind and body. Your outlook can completely change. After this happens, you can be a different person than you were when you lay down, albeit in a small way, but as you know, small changes over a short period of time turn into big changes over blocks of time.

Spell 38: For Invoking Demons to Smite Your Enemies

Oh, please. Grow up. If you turned to this spell looking for answers, you're watching the Sci Fi Channel too much.

Magickal Wisdom: If you ask for the impossible, magick will respond with nonsense.

Hey, just because there's no spell here, don't think you get away without some magickal wisdom. You turned to this spell, so now you need to read why there's no "how to" aspect to this one. The answer is that if you give garbage to the magickal world, it'll respond in kind with nonsense. Demons don't exist. If you ask for something that isn't within the scope of reality, then the spell won't work. Something unpredictable and bad might happen to you, but more likely nothing at all will happen because the magickal world will ignore you. Forget asking for "all the money in the world." Asking for a drop-dead gorgeous dress, that we can do, and you'll find the spell in chapter 7, "The Enchanter: Spells About Dating and Love."

Adeptitude

While having spells for situations in school fills an important need, spellcraft about your interests is downright fun. You should feel good about the spells in this chapter because they relate to the part of your life that drives you forward. No matter where your unique talent lies, be it athletic like soccer, intellectual like chess, or creative like painting, spellcraft will reward you in spades when talent and magick mix.

Back when you collected your tools, you may have noticed that the magick proceeded slowly. You cast the spells and saw the changes happen (you certainly have an athame and wand to show for it), but you weren't about to get a speeding ticket on the psychic highway. The spells have gotten more complicated, and most of them still have a pace that can seem frustratingly slow. If some of them have taken effect quickly, that's mostly your improved skill. But the other piece of the puzzle is that natural energy tends to a gentle rate of change. Magick builds by momentum. It starts slowly and grows over time until it is a force to be reckoned with. The order of spells in this book reflects the deliberate pace of magick so that your magickal growth mirrors the changes you're bringing to your life with each spell you cast and each bit of wisdom you gain. This is partly why I recommend casting spells slowly rather than one right after another. Your body and the web of energy both need time to build momentum for magick to occur.

How can you make your spells gain in intensity?

By momentum. **Spells gain in intensity as magick builds momentum.**

With the gradual pace of magickal change, it's crucial to know that you can increase its intensity when you need to. Or you can decrease it. In order to add to the momentum that magick builds, you will also need to answer the question: What can you do to make your magick the most effective possible? The answer will be revealed in the upcoming pages when you read about becoming a diviner.

CHAPTER 5

THE DIVINER: SPELLS ABOUT HOME AND FAMILY

NOW WE MOVE ON to spells related to your home environment. From the security of your bedroom to the familiar smells in your kitchen, home can bring you comfort and peace. And home of course wouldn't be the same without your family members who encourage you as well as remind you of your responsibilities. Each one of us gets an important part of his or her personal identity from growing up in a family. Close interaction with each member of your family, mother, father, and siblings, influences you over the years as you develop.

But living closely with people and sharing both space, such as bathrooms and family rooms, and objects, such as the refrigerator and television, can have its challenges. So, in this chapter you'll find spells to deal with siblings, to help you talk to your parents, and to dispel discord. Sooner or later your family will change, perhaps when a sibling goes off to college or in the less fortunate event of a divorce, and when this separation comes, there's a spell to ease the new dynamic at home. Of course, you'll get more magickal wisdom under your belt along the way that builds on the previous ones. Even if some spells don't initially seem to be relevant to you, you'll find that they come up later on and that the wisdom from each will strengthen the spells you do cast.

You'll also notice that the points of magickal wisdom delve into your spiritual growth. They're no longer just rules to follow. They're showing you how you can change your mind for magickal work and change the quality of your life in the process. I mention this because one of the magickal wisdom points that you'll learn in this chapter is about personal issues that'll come up for you. It's usually when dealing with family relations that the spiritual world strikes hardest with showing you the kinks in your personality that need to be examined and changed somehow. If you have the right outlook and undertake this work, you'll find that you've a new understanding of your family members and better relationships with them than ever before. You're divining for hidden water, strengthening the already positive, loving emotions you share with your family. You'll also find your ability to work with magick improves when you address these personal issues.

By casting these spells and internalizing the magickal wisdom points, you'll become adept in the matters of the diviner. You'll learn what you can do to make magick the most effective possible.

Here is your grounding and centering meditation for the spells in this chapter. It's called the "inner light" meditation, and it's about feeling the energy within you, the same life force that pushes you to do the best you can and reach your full potential as a person. It's not so hard to do, but the influence it can have on you is great, which is why I've put it in a later chapter. The more you try to reflect your own inner light, the more all people, most especially you, will see the positive intent behind all that you do.

Grounding and Centering Meditation: The Inner Light

Take a deep breath, and as you exhale, picture light in your core as a small glowing sphere around your solar plexus (the hollow between your belly button and the bottom of your ribs). Now picture the glow enlarging.

Take another deep breath, and as you let it out, gradually picture the glow encompassing your insides and stretching up to your heart and down to your pubic region. Picture the glow gathering strength and intensity as it reaches up to your head, extends down your legs, and climbs out your arms. As the perimeter of your body feels the light, imagine your skin receiving that glow.

Take a deep breath, and when you exhale, let the light emanate outward from your body. Now pull the light up from the ground through your feet and send the light out of your head as a ray to the sky. Watch as light spills from above your head down to

the ground where you see it coming up through your feet again. Continue to breathe evenly and feel the warmth and vibrancy of this light encompassing you.
When you feel inner calmness, you're ready to start your work.

Here is how to cast the circle for the spells in this chapter. The "Stages of Life" method of casting the circle, and calling quarters is similar to the seasons' method in the last chapter, "The Socerer: Spells About Fun, Sports, and Hobbies," but it specifically addresses people rather than plants. We play roles throughout life at various ages, and as such, it's closer to home. It places you in the cycle of life where you've been, where you are now, and where you're going.

Circle Casting: The Stages of Life

Begin by holding your athame in your dominant hand and cup your nondominant hand around your dominant hand. Focus pulling energy up from the earth through yourself and send that energy out of the athame toward the north. Push it out so that it continues to the east. Keep driving it out so that it goes to the south. Direct it to the west. Propel it north, and keep thrusting it around the circle a second time and then a third time. When you have a solid circle, thank your athame, and put it down.
Take your wand and face north. Stand for a moment quietly and then turn to face the east.

Still facing the east, say, "I honor the son and
daughter, the child in all of us."

Turn to the south, and say, "I honor the lover and
beloved, the adolescent in all of us."

Turn to the west, and say, "I honor the mother and
father, the parent in all of us."

Turn to the north, and say, "I honor the crone and
consort, the elder in all of us."

Go back to center and say, "I have arrived between
the worlds." You're ready to begin.

The Spells

Spell 39: For Sibling Relations

YOU WILL NEED:

three twigs

roll of blue yarn

wad of clay

Brothers and sisters can be your best friends in a pinch
or a nuisance when you least need it. Any close relationship is going to have its difficulties at some time, but you
know you can fall back on your family ties when you need
them. Concentrate on minimizing the tough times and
increasing the good times.

As you prepare for this spell, think about the behavior
and situations with your siblings that bother you the most.
If you have a younger sibling, you may be getting pestered
to pay attention and play with him or her. It can be really

annoying when you want to do something yourself. Stop a moment and think about why your younger brother or sister is acting this way. It's probably because he or she looks up to you. He or she doesn't mean to be a pest. If you have an older brother or sister, he or she may be teasing you or beating you up. Stop a moment and think about why this might be happening. It's possible that someone bigger or stronger than your older brother is giving him a hard time. It's possible that your older sister is having trouble with her friends. It's not fair for them to take out their difficulties on you, but sometimes it happens.

Despite irritations and annoyances, all of you share the same parents. Even if you're adopted or you have step-siblings or stepparents, those adults love and care for all of you. Your life will be smoother if you find a way to acknowledge your similarities and make peace with these relationships at least while you're living together. Your siblings will also probably respond well if you treat them as respected individuals. That's the way you like to be treated, right?

Family relationships can be intense because you're all living together. You're sharing a relatively small space, and it's not because you want to. Concentrate on the cooperation people need to have to live together.

As you look for the three twigs, choose sturdy twigs that are relatively straight and at least 12, preferably 18, inches long. Think of the twigs as the physical ties that connect you to your siblings. As you look for the yarn, choose an aqua shade of blue to represent the sea of emotions that bonds family members. It's even better if you can find a skein that repeats a change from blue to green and back again.

The Spell: Ground and center. Cast the circle.

Take a deep breath and sit quietly for another moment to think of some of the negative feelings you've had after difficult experiences with your siblings. There have probably been many of them. Each time you think of one, exhale a long breath. Let it out. All siblings have squabbles. Concentrate on the feelings behind your differences. Relax and let them go. Focus on your feelings so that you're not focusing on blaming with phrases such as "He said that!" or "She did this to me!" Calm yourself. You're doing this spell for yourself, not anyone else. When you've done this enough so that you feel still and gentle—and that you've released some of the tension from your woes—use your hands to wrap up that energy in a ball and roll the ball to North. Give North that energy to recycle.

Now turn your focus in a calm, yet determined, way to the positive. Think about the connections, similarities, and positive bonds you have with your siblings. Concentrate on the feelings you get from those. Don't bother about praising him or her. Stay on focus: you. When did you have experiences with them that made you feel appreciation, happiness, and love? Stay with these warm feelings.

Take your three twigs. Say, "Twigs, poles that symbolize the stability of the Earth, I charge you to hold my web." Now take your twigs and make a six-prong star so that they all meet in a common center. Use the clay to keep the center solid. It will harden over time, but for now you need enough strength to keep the twigs in place while you work with the yarn.

Pick up the skein of yarn, and say, "Yarn, you are blue green like the sea, the sea with its strong tide, I charge you with the power of emotions that are both fierce and gentle." Tie the end of the yarn to the end of one of the twigs. String the yarn from that tied end to the next spoke clockwise and wrap the yarn around it. Keep doing this until you reach the center. It should look like a spider web. You do not need to have each ring positioned tightly next to the previous one, but you can do that if you like. I prefer to vary it. As you weave this web, you may want to chant a gentle, lulling song. Make up the notes as you go. Here are lyrics I like to chant: "Weaving a web of understanding, weaving a web of feeling, weaving a web of connection, weaving my spiral toward the center."

When you're done, hold the web in your hands. Stand up and face the web to the west. Say, "I honor my connection to others, and I acknowledge my feelings. I will try to be peaceful through difficulty with my siblings. I will try to strengthen happiness with my siblings." Keep the web on your altar or somewhere where it won't be jostled.

Devoke and put your hands together and blow air outward through them. As you do, let the extra energy of the circle whoosh down into the ground.

If you want to add a charm in the center later on, I suggest a picture of a dove, and best if you create it yourself.

Magickal Wisdom: Avoid manipulative magick by careful planning before casting a spell.

The process of creating a spell involves getting all the particulars straight beforehand so that you've thought about what you're going to do in your circle. Thinking of a specific person during this planning process isn't manipulative magick. You need to think about the specific person and events and tendencies in order to figure out what to do in your spell so that it's not manipulative. As you already know, it's not okay to include a specific person in the magick you do during the spell. Figuring out how to prevent manipulative magick, however, is an important step.

Spell 40: Against Family Discord

YOU WILL NEED:

light purple cord 3 feet long

12 jingle bells

Every family has discord occasionally. Every family has infrequent stressful events, such as births, deaths, marriages, and some families seem to have continual tension. Concentrate on promoting ongoing harmony in your home.

As you prepare for this spell, think about how nice it is to live in a peaceful environment in which each family member feels supported, loved, nurtured, and valued as an individual. You may have trouble doing this if you're working on the spell in the middle of a stressful situation rather than as a preventative measure, but stick with it. Move your mind to that place where you can see harmony and balance in your home. Remember times when your parents praised you, when your family was happy and laughing. It's easiest to do this when you visualize yourself in the physical surroundings. Leave other family members out of this spell.

In choosing the cord, look for a light purple, violet, or lilac that's pleasing and restful in color. Purple is associated with deep healing and deep inner spirituality. Explain what you're about to do, and ask the cord if it wants to be part of your magickal spell. It's easier to know when it doesn't want to participate than when it does. A "No" will be strong, and a "Yes" may be gentler. You'll know it when you feel it. Choose bells that are all the same type and have a pleasing sound when they ring.

The Spell: Ground and center. Cast the circle.

Sit on the ground and hold your light purple cord so that each hand has one end. Say, "As energy flows through me, so, too, it flows through this cord."

Make a loop on one end of the cord and knot it tight. Then add a bell near the loop at the top of the cord and knot it in place. Do this with each of the rest of the bells at an equal distance from each other (the exact distance will depend on how much of the cord is left after you've made the loop). When all the bells are knotted in, crumble bay leaves over them. When the spell is done, the sound of the bells will stimulate harmony in your home, and the bay leaves, which correspond with your sense of hearing, will intensify the bells' power to create harmony.

Chant an "ah" sound for a long time in a comfortable, medium tone. Keep it going, stopping only to inhale deeply. Say, "As I vibrate peace throughout this circle, let this string of bells ring out balance and harmony throughout my home. So mote it be." Ring the bells.

Devoke, and end by ringing the bells again to ground the energy.

Hang the bells anywhere in the house where you'll see them. Jiggle the cord and listen to their sound whenever you want a wave of peace and harmony. If anyone else rings them, they're adding to this spell's work without knowing it. Even if you have a calm home, ringing the bells will strengthen it further.

Magickal Wisdom: Magick urges you to confront your faults.

As you work magick, you will notice your buttons getting pushed. Working magick tends to bring up your issues, to press you to confront your shortcomings as a person. These are the knots in your personality that get in your way. I've put this wisdom with the spell about family discord because family members can get on your nerves in a way that few others can. And it's hard to avoid them. Much as you love them, and admit it, deep down you do, they can get you angry in a flash. If you examine yourself closely, difficult though this is, you may find that family members are the origin or trigger of many of your personal faults. Figuring out what aspects of yourself hinder you will free you. You can't control other people's actions, but you can control yours. The more you address these personal issues, the more effective your magickal work will be.

Spell 41: For Explaining Difficult Matters to Parents

YOU WILL NEED:
  yellow candle
  white candle
  matches
  table fork
  aluminum foil or other nonflammable surface

At some point in your life, you and your parents will sit you down to talk. Maybe they won't be happy about something, and they'll ask you to explain just what exactly you were thinking and doing. Or maybe you need to persuade them about something. If so, you're going to need to explain how important it is to you and why. You want them to take you seriously.

As you prepare for this spell, think about how family "talks" can involve a lot of parental talking and very little time for you to talk. They can also involve a lot of advice for you. Take a deep breath. Once you acknowledge this, it will help you deal with it.

You need good communication in this situation. That means you need to be clear and concise in what you say because you may not have a lot of time to say it. You will also be doing some listening as your parents talk. And you hope that they will keep an open mind about you and listen to you. You have convincing to do.

As you choose the two candles, concentrate on calling for listening and calling for good communication. It's best if these candles are tapers, long and thin, but votive candles will be fine too. The fork should feel comfortable to hold, and it should have strong tines since you'll be using them to carve into the candle wax.

The Spell: Ground and center. Cast the circle. Really focus on East. This spirit (East) and its corresponding attributes are going to be important in this spell.

Take a deep breath before beginning your magickal work. Concentrate on clarity and sharing information. Say, "I cast this spell for good communication. I ask for a meaningful exchange during which I listen and speak and during which I am heard and I am understood."

Take another deep breath, and place your candles in front of you. Pick up the yellow one, and say the following incantation, "I carve good communication into this candle for speaking and being understood and for listening and being heard." As you say this, use the fork to carve this symbol in three places on the candle: △ This is the symbol for Air that corresponds to the direction East and the power of communication. Do the same with the white candle and keep repeating that incantation.

The next part is somewhat tricky and could be dangerous, so be very careful doing it. Using a match over the nonflammable surface, melt one long side of the yellow candle and one long side of the white candle. Push them together so that they bond. This needs to be done somewhat quickly because the wax cools very fast. Don't worry about the blackness that appears when the wax melts. It is unavoidable.

Practical note: You're dealing with fire in this spell, so if anything starts to get out of control, stop your spell to deal with it. If the match burns down and your fingers start to get warm, blow out the match and start with a new one. It may take time to join the candles together, and that's fine. It's better to prevent a fire and start the spell later than to risk burning down the house or burning yourself.

Next, stand holding your two candles, and say, "By the power of East and Air, I charge this yellow candle with listening and hearing with being heard and being understood. I charge this white candle with the purity of intention and the power to magnify a worthy goal. I desire good communication after burning these candles in tandem."

Light the two candles and watch them burn together. Know that you have a strong opportunity for heartfelt communication with your parents. Be willing to hear them out, but be equally willing to share important information about yourself with them.

Devoke, and end by snapping your fingers.

Magickal Wisdom: Interpretation is a spiritual act.

Life would be so much easier if we received spiritual

messages that told us what to do. But it's never that simple. As it is, we all spend considerable time deliberating about what to do in various situations from the mundane "When can I fit in a run to the supermarket?" to the more emotional "How do I deal tactfully with my parents?" For the more weighty of these deliberations, it's appropriate to ask for spiritual guidance (gosh, I hope you don't need this sort of guidance for when to go to the supermarket), and you will receive it. Here's the catch. Usually, you will get the message in a filtered way so that you can't understand it easily. It's up to you to figure out what it means and how it applies to your work. And this interpretation leads to your spiritual growth. It's part of the process, and it's supposed to work that way. Have you ever noticed in fantasy books that the hero is challenged with a riddle that seems like nonsense until he figures it out? The spiritual messages are a different sort of riddle that you will need to puzzle through. But once you do, the answer will seem so obvious that you should've seen it from the beginning.

Spell 42: For Preventing Others from Eating Your Food in the Fridge

YOU WILL NEED:

   privacy with the refrigerator
   pebble or ice cube

The refrigerator is a public space for your whole family, and if you are not standing there to stop them, family members may consume food you put there without asking whose it is. Concentrate on preserving your food so it will be there when you return for it.

As you prepare for this spell, you will need to concentrate on the food that you want to protect. Have this food clearly in mind. Have a strong sense of connection to this food. Maybe you made the food or a friend gave it to you or you took it home as leftovers from a restaurant. Also, think about the refrigerator and about how it is an inanimate object with a personality. It probably makes some sort of humming noise as it cools its contents. It has energy powering it, as it's plugged into the wall and needs electricity to make it run. It has a door that opens and closes and probably drawers, shelves, and knobs that are moveable on the inside. Think about the rhythm of the refrigerator's days and its purpose.

The Spell: Go up to the fridge, and stand in front of it. Ground and center. Cast the circle.

Open the door. Look inside. Close the door. Place the palms of your hands on the door. Say, "Refrigerator, you steady the worlds of hot and cold. You serve and protect what is put in you."

Gently tap the palms of your hands on the door. Create a rhythm. Pum, pum, pum, pa-pum. Pum, pum, pum, pa-pum. Pum, pum, pum, pa-pum. Pum, pum, pum, pa-pum. Keep up this rhythm for a while. Build it into a regular sort of heartbeat for the fridge. Say, "We put our food in your belly, but you do not consume it."

Keep up your tapping rhythm: pum, pum, pum, pa-pum;

pum, pum, pum, pa-pum. Say, "Refrigerator, I come to you out of respect. I come to you to ask for your help. You keep food for other people. You keep food for any of us to eat. But when I put my food in you, please save it only for me. When I put my food in you, please keep it until I return for it. Protect my food."

To end the spell, say that last line "protect my food" three times. Then make a loud last round of pum, pum, pum, *Pa-pum.* Put the pebble or ice cube in the refrigerator as a gift to it for the work it will do for you. Try to put it in a place where it's not so noticeable to other people such as the back of a drawer or in a far corner. Leave it in for some time after you've taken out your food, but eventually take the pebble or ice cube (if it hasn't melted) out.

Devoke.

Note that this spell isn't intended to claim food that would otherwise be available for everyone to eat. It's only for food that's specifically yours. Also, remember the locker spell? These spells are similar in that you're protecting something inside of both the locker and the refrigerator. There's an important difference, however, in that the locker spell seals the door so that nobody can go in and the refrigerator spell only protects what's yours inside a place other people access.

Magickal Wisdom: Every spirit has needs.

The refrigerator, like every other object and being in the world, has a spirit. By casting this spell, you acknowledge the fridge's spirit, and it'll begin to communicate with you. When you ask a spirit for something, it has the right to ask for something in return and may do so. You'll begin an ongoing relationship with the fridge as a separate being. This doesn't mean that it'll start speaking to you or opening its doors by itself. Every once in a while, you may have an out-of-the-blue thought about the fridge such as "Come get something in here" or "Could you please move the ketchup to the other shelf." First of all, recognize that this isn't just a random thought you're having. This is the refrigerator trying to contact you the only way that it knows how. You may not understand why the fridge is asking for what it wants, but for some reason, it'll feel the need for a shift of some sort. It's reaching out to you because you reached out to it. Second, you're in a relationship now; it gives you what you ask for, and in return, it will occasionally ask you for things. When you honor the fridge's requests, you will find it happy to oblige with yours.

Spell 43: For Softening Punishment Before the Punishment Is Given

YOU WILL NEED:
  candle
  disposable cup
  pen
  cup of milk
  large bowl

As you prepare for this spell, you will probably be anxious. All you can think about is what you would've, could've, should've done to avoid being caught. At this point that's in the past. Now you need to concentrate on diminishing your punishment. Try to take that worry and send it away. Your mind may be racing with images as you replay events repeatedly. Your body may be shaky. Try to find some tranquility in your body and quiet in your mind. Release the jitters and send them into the ground. While you collect the items that you'll need, you'll want to be in balance within yourself as much as possible.

Find a pen that can write well on a disposable cup. It can have a thick or thin point. The important part is that disposable cups can have a waxy finish on them that is difficult to write on. Regular whole milk is best for this spell because it contains some fat, which has richness not found in 2% or skim milk. But in a pinch, milk is milk. The milk shouldn't be in the disposable cup. First, put it in the cup that you keep on your altar.

You will also need a bowl big enough to collect the milk while moving the milk in a circular motion during the spell. In this spell the bowl represents Earth, so look for a bowl that reminds you of that. Maybe you have a bowl of rough clay or one that is brown.

The Spell: Ground and center. Cast the circle. Light the candle.

Pick up the disposable cup. On one side of it write your offense, the reason you're up for punishment. For example, you could write, "I punched Joe," "I got caught drinking," or "I failed my science test." Write a full sentence with "I" at the beginning of it. Even if your infringement involves someone else, forget about others and concentrate just on yourself. If your cup is the sort with a wax covering over it, you'll have difficulty writing on it with a pen. Try scratching the wax with your fingernail. On the other side of the cup write, "This milk is spilled already."

Hold your altar cup with the milk in it. Look into the cup at the creamy whiteness of the milk. Softly blow air onto the surface of the milk and watch as it changes from a smooth surface to a rippled surface. Visualize your energy, as calm as possible, moving on the surface of the milk carried by your breath.

Pour some milk from the cup you keep on your altar about halfway into the disposable cup. Lift the cup up, and chant, "The milk spilled but it wasn't sour yet. Lessen any punishment that I may get."

Making a counterclockwise circular motion, pour all the milk from your disposable cup into your bowl that is circular like the earth, made of clay. The idea is that you are using your powerful energy to direct the milk into the earth (represented here by the bowl) where the spilled milk will be transformed for a positive purpose. Visualize this happening as the milk is sinking into the ground or flowing down the drain to the earth. Say, "It is so."

Devoke. Jump up and down with both feet three times and clap your hands together once.

Later take all the milk in the bowl and pour it outside on the ground or at the very least into a sink using a counter-clockwise motion and continue to visualize the milk returning to the earth.

Magickal Wisdom: Magick will try to put you in the right place for your next step.

Magickal work will change you as well as cause the change you request in your spell. The change you see in yourself after casting a spell is the first step in the change you have set in motion with your spell. Casting this spell will start a process going. The first part of that process will be some relief or a change in attitude that you feel within yourself after casting the spell. This does not lessen the effect of the spell. If anything, this change in you will strengthen the spell. You will be more ready and able to act differently in the mundane world when facing your parents or teachers or whoever is supposed to sit you down, talk to you, and punish you. By grounding and centering, by casting the circle and calling the quarters, and by focusing your entire being on the spell, you have changed from the state you were in before you began. This physical and emotional change can benefit you. Perhaps it will allow you to explain yourself more clearly and succinctly than before. Perhaps your demeanor will change just enough so that you will act more maturely. In addition to the change that the spell will cause, you will change because you have worked magick.

Spell 44: For Easing a Separation

YOU WILL NEED:

light blue modeling clay
5-inch circle of pink paper
blue pen
white candle
matches

At some point there will be a separation in your family. Sometimes these separations come earlier than expected, such as when parents divorce, and sometimes this natural process happens as kids grow up and go off to live on their own. Separation is not easy because there will be a new family dynamic for the people who are still living in the space without the person who used to be around.

As you prepare for this spell, concentrate on your family as a whole and on how one member has gone or will go away, but you will still be a family. Perhaps the person will be gone only temporarily as in a sibling to summer camp. If this is a long-term change such as divorce, there may be intense feelings of anger as well as adjustment. Death is a final separation and will take the longest to sink in. (In this case I suggest indigo modeling clay because indigo corresponds to the third eye and psychic communication. I also recommend a follow-up visit to a grief counselor.)

The Spell: Ground and center. Cast the circle.

Breathe deeply in the center of your room. Light your

white candle, and let the purity and peace it stands for permeate your circle and yourself.

Take out the modeling clay and use your thumbs and palms to knead it until it is soft and warm. Visualize the happy times when your family has been all together as you do this. Sprinkle some cinnamon in the clay to trigger your sense of smell which provides a fast connection to that comforting smell of home. When you are ready, divide the clay into the number of people in your family. (If you have a mother and father, brother and sister, there are five in total in your family, so divide the clay into five equal sections.) Begin to form five balls of the same size with the clay so that each ball can represent anyone in your family. As you do, the cinnamon should disappear within the clay. Do not think about a specific member of the family corresponding to each ball. If you do, you will tread dangerously close to the fine line between ethical magick and unethical, manipulative magick. Another way I like to do this is by forming the clay into birds so that I can figuratively see the birds of my family in a nest together. But either way, balls or birds, will work fine.

Put the clay balls (or birds) together on your altar in a circle. Keep in mind the light blue color that promotes tranquility at home.

Take out your 5-inch circle of pink paper, and draw a heart on it with the blue pen. Say, "May all my family be covered and supported by love no matter where each person is. May I keep my connection with each one." Place the circle on top of the clay balls (or birds). Here you are reinforcing warmth and love.

I suggest that you sit calmly for at least a few minutes more before blowing out the candle while you feel the bond you share with each person. When you're done, say, "So mote it be."

Devoke.

Magickal Wisdom: Change, even for positive reasons, is stressful.

As human beings, we like stability in our lives. Routine gives us security because we know what to expect. Many people are afraid of the dark, which is actually a fear of the unseen and therefore the unknown and unexpected. We all will go through changes. Many changes are good ones, including marriages, and new births, and even going to a new school can be positive. Good changes, however, are still difficult and take adjustment. Many changes are unhappy surprises such as death of a pet, parent, grand-parent, or friend. When working magick, you're opening yourself up to change. Be easy on yourself through the process of change. Try to create smooth transitions for yourself whenever possible.

Spell 45: For Invisibility

YOU WILL NEED:

a calm, clear mind

Sometimes you don't want people to find you. Maybe you need to do something or you're busy and you don't want to be bothered. Maybe you can tell that someone is in a bad mood. Whatever the reason, concentrate on your desire to go unnoticed.

As you prepare for this spell, think about Air for a moment. How do you know Air is there? You see things moving in it, but you don't see air itself. You see dust in a mote of sun. You see fallen leaves blowing along the ground or branches swaying. Think also about how you sometimes feel as if someone is there who, when you turn your head, isn't there at all. And sometimes you have no idea that someone has come up to you when you're not paying attention. You'll be dealing with this type of perception and your own body in this spell. As you're working on this, become very centered and calm. These feelings are crucial in this spell.

The Spell: Ground and center. Cast the circle.

Sit calmly with your hands on your knees. Breathe five long, deep breaths. Go as slowly as you can. Breathe in and exhale.

Visualize yourself. In your mind, picture your body and all its solid parts, your head, your legs, your arms, and your torso. Gradually, visualize your body as the outline of your physical self. Your solid body is beginning to fade away and your spirit body is what is left.

Visualize air blowing around your spirit self, swirling and picking up speed. Now visualize the air moving through you and mixing with your breath. Now visualize the air moving anywhere as if you were not there. You feel wispy, as if you had no need to move your physical body as the energy in the swirling air builds. Then visualize the air moving slowly through you as if all it were doing was moving dust in a mote of light. The air wafts through your body as if it were floating and you weren't there.

When you're done with being invisible, devoke. Do something to ground yourself well such as taking a nap or eating.

You can do this spell anywhere you like because it doesn't have words, spoken or written, or ingredients or tools. It is purely about changing your state of mind. And while you won't actually turn into thin air, the results will be as if you had.

Magickal Wisdom: Be conscious of the footprint you leave behind.

The spirit world rewards those who honor it and give more than they take. Think about what you leave behind in order to live. When you are gone, when you are only a spirit and are physically invisible, what evidence remains that you ever existed? What space do you take up as a person? What waste do you produce? Sure, everyone goes to the bathroom, but we also discard lots of trash when we are finished eating, when discarding old clothes, and when moving from one house to another. What resources do you consume in order to live? How much liquid do you drink? How much food do you eat? What about clothes and housing?

You depend on the earth for the resources you need to live. Are you careful not to be wasteful or to produce more waste than necessary? If you work with natural earth energy, and by casting these spells you are, then you need to think about the balance in your relationship with the earth. What are you giving back? What difference are you making in the world? We all have different ways of honoring the earth. Some people become involved in politics, while others become absorbed in charity work. Are you trying your best to be a decent person and live a good life? Are you thankful for what you have? Do you appreciate what others do for you? Work toward decreasing what you leave behind and increasing what you give.

Adeptitude

When you're close to something, it's hard to have an objective perspective about it. That is certainly true of family issues. Family can be both supportive and tense, and the spells in this chapter with the accompanying wisdom sections aren't all easy, so give yourself credit for the magick you've done recently. You've probably taken a hard look at who you are in relation to your family.

Nevertheless, you have some impressive magick under your belt. You've no doubt cast some spells that somehow involve other people without breaking any ethics about manipulative magick. You're promoting harmony at home as well as increasing your communication about what matters to you. And you've tried the sought-after invisibility spell that will serve you well from this day forward. Have you noticed that spells seem to make a greater impact lately? Think back, and consider that, because I'll bet you have.

Trickier changes may be happening more easily. Yes, you've built momentum with your magick by now, but something else is going on. You've allowed magick to flow in the easiest manner possible. How is that? Magick supports the changes you want when you're working toward your spiritual growth. If any of your personal issues came up and you dealt with them, you'll see that the web of energy wants you to succeed. You'll receive encouragement in the form of more return from your spellcraft. You'll work with the web of energy rather than against it, and your spells will have extra vigor.

What can you do to make your magick the most effective possible?

Grow spiritually. **Working toward your spiritual growth makes your magick the most effective possible.**

Now that you've built momentum and are working with, rather than against, the web of energy with the spells you cast, you may think it's time to open your own magick shop. Are you ready to tackle any kind of spell? Almost. In order to do so, you will need to answer the following question: What is the greatest law of magick? When you do, you'll be ready to cast spells with friends, not just for them, but with them. Charge ahead and let your days as a charmer be fruitful.

CHAPTER 6

THE CHARMER: SPELLS ABOUT FRIENDS

THIS CHAPTER OF SPELLS involving friendship is a big reward for getting through the tough emotions of the previous chapter. But the good news is that you made it and are forging ahead. Your friends are people that you like to spend time with. You share yourself with them, and they reciprocate. You help when they need it, and they help when you need it. Besides that, they make the journey so much more satisfying than going it alone. As an aside, if you're lucky, you may consider your family members friends as well. Just because you're related by blood doesn't mean you dislike each other. And as for friends with whom you share equally close emotional ties but are not bound by blood, we call these "family by choice" because you choose these strong bonds.

You have probably noticed that many of the spells throughout the book address emotions. If you're putting your emotions into each spell, you're increasing the impact that you'll cause. This chapter and the next, "The Enchanter: Spells about Dating and Love," are linked because you share deep emotional bonds with the people you love, both friends and romantic partners. So these will be intense and powerful spells. Nevertheless, when emotions are involved, you have a personal investment in what happens. And if a relationship gets troublesome, it can wreak havoc in your heart. For this reason, I suggest that you proceed carefully with each spell. Whereas before I suggested that you cast no more than one spell per day, at this point I suggest that you slow down and cast no more than one spell every three days. Changes take time to happen, and although some of the results will happen quickly, most will take time to develop and take effect in the world.

A big step for you in this chapter is that there are a few spells to do with a friend. Your friend must take part with you willingly. Be careful how you present the idea of casting a spell to your friend. He or she may not be open to the idea initially, and when you start talking about magick and spells, some people will think you're crazy. Choose an appropriate time, and find a private place for your discussion. If you talk about magick, you become a dignitary and spokesperson for all people who practice magick. Remember people will see your views on these subjects in the way that you present yourself and how you say it as well as by what you say. If your friend doesn't want to do a spell with you, don't force the issue. If he or she reacts poorly to the whole topic, it's best to back off quickly. You will find friends with a common interest someday.

You'll notice that the magickal wisdom sections have become more intense. Give them time to settle in, as they carry profound messages that need to sink into the core of your being. So now you're off to be your charming self and to do some important magickal work.

Here is your grounding and centering meditation for the spells in this chapter. It's the heartbeat meditation, which is exactly what it sounds like—you feel your heart beating. You live with this motion every day, and yet we are so busy moving our bodies that we rarely stop to listen to our own internal rhythm. Each time you go through this grounding and centering process, concentrate on your heart and take time to connect to and appreciate your own internal ticking.

Grounding and Centering Meditation: The Heartbeat

Stand tall and turn your attention to your heart. Feel your heart. Try to feel it beating. If you need to feel your pulse by putting your hand on your wrist or neck, that is fine.

Take a deep breath. Feel how your breath changes the rhythm of your heart. As you exhale, continue to pay attention to the beating.

Take another deep breath, and concentrate on your own internal rhythm as you exhale. As your heart beats, feel your own energy emanating from your heart and being carried throughout your body. Feel the rhythm and energy of your own body supporting you, sustaining you.

Take another deep breath. Slowly exhale. Feel your whole body working in tune with itself. Feel how you are part of the whole world, that your inner heartbeat reflects the world around you and that you belong in this place. You are an integral part of the world. When you feel this connection, start your magickal work as you please.

Here is how to cast the circle for the spells in this chapter. Every person, no matter what age, has friends. Connecting with other people is one of the benefits of being human. Actually, I think it's more than that. I think communicating and connecting with other people allow us to feel that life has purpose and meaning, that each time we help someone we feel that we're here for a reason.

It's the wide range of emotions that makes us feel good or bad and that guides us through life, rewarding us with positive feelings or steering us away from situations that feel negative. By casting the circle and calling the quarters with this method based on emotions, you will heighten your own feelings within the circle and enhance your magick. It's not for beginners because emotions are not always easy to manage, but you will ultimately benefit from using this method.

Circle Casting: The Emotions

Stand in the center and point your athame north.
Then move it to face east as if you were drawing an arc from north to east. Then continue with another arc from east to south. Then continue with another arc from south to west. Then continue another arc from west to north so that the four arcs make a

complete circle around the space where you are working. Then turn around with your athame pointing but do not stop at each quarter. Do this a third time. Finally, it is okay to put your athame down and pick up your wand.

Stand holding your wand in the center. Then walk to face each direction starting silently in the north.

Turn to the east, and say, "East, as I breathe in, bring me inspiration in this sacred space."

Turn to the south, and say, "South, as I direct my will, lend me passion in this sacred space."

Turn to the west, and say, "West, as I feel, allow me wisdom in this sacred space."

Turn to the north, and say, "North, as I move, give me security in this sacred space."

Your circle is cast, and you will have emotional balance in this world between the worlds.

The Spells

Spell 46: For Attracting a New Friend

YOU WILL NEED:

2 leaves that come from the same tree
string

As you prepare for this spell, think about the importance of friends in your life. You are preparing to call a new person into your life, someone you do not know or at least someone whom you do not already identify as a friend. Think about why you want a new friend. Do you have a new pastime that you want to enjoy with someone so that the two of you can do it together? Do you have classes with no friends, so you want someone to study with? Or are you ready for a new perspective and new energy in your life? In finding a new friend, think about the qualities you like in a friend. What are you looking for in this person and in your new relationship with this person? Think about the qualities you want to attract into your life.

Choose two leaves from the same tree, not just the same kind of tree, but both from the same tree. To be sure you have leaves from the same tree, you will have to take both leaves from the same fallen branch or take two still attached to the tree. The leaves should have stems on them. Even a stub of a stem is okay. Ask the leaves for permission before taking them. The string should be pink or white for friendship and about 3 feet long.

The Spell: Ground and center. Cast the circle.

Stand in the center of your circle, and hold both leaves, one in each hand. Say, "Here are two leaves. Each leaf is separate and individual. But at one point they were on the same tree, connected by common roots." Put the leaves down on your altar.

Sit down and hold the string with one end in each hand and stretch it out. Visualize energy building up in your hands and traveling back and forth down the string. Let it vibrate with warm energy. Say, "The warmth of friendship and kindness runs from each end down this string, so that it is not just a string but a pathway from one good friend to another."

Then tie one end of the string to one leaf's stem, and say, "Knot of one, the work is done." Tie the other end of the string to the other leaf's stem, and say, "Knot of two, the work is true." If your rosemary is in twig form, tie a piece of it to the middle of the string between the two leaves. If you've got loose rosemary, crumble them in your fingers and rub them on the two leaves so that the leaves smell like rosemary. This will heighten your sense of sight in the spell so that you recognize the new friend when you see him or her.

Then stand up and hold each leaf in one hand. Say, "These two leaves are separate and individual. Yet they came from one common tree and shared the same root connection. Two friends are leaves on a tree, sharing a common root system and connecting for one ultimate purpose. May I find my new friend, may he or she travel the easy road of root connection to me, and may we make our lives better, happier, and more fun for the greater good of all." Put the leaves together, and wrap the string around the two stems to join the leaves. Then say, "So mote it be."

Devoke.

You may want to pin the leaves on a bulletin board if you have one in your room or put them on your altar.

Magickal Wisdom: Make sure that you honestly want what you are asking for.

Getting what you want means taking the responsibility for receiving it, so make sure you're ready to receive what you ask for after you do the spell. If the web of the world gives you an opportunity, it'll want you to take it and make the most of it. If you waste what is given to you, you may not receive what you ask for the next time. In the case of this spell, you're asking for a new friend. Do you have time and energy for a new friend? A friendship is a give and take relationship, and if you call someone to you because you need help, expect that you'll need to keep up the relationship and help your new friend when requested. I don't mean to turn you off casting this spell. I mean to warn you to think seriously about the implications surrounding each spell before you set the web of energy in motion.

Spell 47: For Communicating Something Important

YOU WILL NEED:
   white paper
   gold paper
   red pen
   glue
   blue cord
   small piece of wire or wire loop

When you have something important to say, you want people to pay attention and listen to you. Most people do not tell other people their dreams, goals, and great hopes in life. Because our dreams matter so much personally, we guard them closely as secrets. Yours might be that you want to be a veterinarian one day and help animals. Or maybe you want to make music and have people all over the world listen to it. Or maybe you want to find your soul mate and fall in love. Concentrate on how valuable matters of the heart are and how vulnerable they make you.

As you find the paper, pens, and cord you will need, think about what it is that you have in your heart. What is important to you. What do you want to become a reality or what matters to you. In other words, what do you want to say? To whom do you want to say it? Consider what reaction you might get and what reaction you want when you share this information. You may have a detailed idea of what you want or an elaborate plan of how to do it. Or it could be something really simple. Whatever it is, try to get to the core essence of what your heart-matter is.

Before you start the spell, cut a heart shape out of the white paper. It should be no more than 1 inch at the widest space. Cut a heart out of the gold paper, but make it slightly larger than the white heart.

The Spell: Ground and center. Cast the circle.

Say, "Matters of the heart matter a great deal."

Put your hands over your heart. Feel it beating. Tell your heart that you recognize its importance. "Heart, I care about you and what you feel." Then move your hands to your throat and lightly put them where your Adam's apple is. This is an energy center called the throat chakra.

Visualize the blue circle of swirling energy there. This chakra controls your communication, which is no surprise since you use your voice box and throat to convey sounds.

Next sit down and use the red pen full of active energy to write down your heart's passion, the important statement you want to make. Write it on the cutout white heart. Then stand up and say it aloud.

Next, glue the white heart to the gold heart so that the red writing is hidden between them forever. What you should have left is a white heart that has a gold rim around it. Press the heart against your throat, and let out a loud "ah" sound. Let the vibration of that sound fill the paper heart.

Poke a small hole in the heart so that you can put a metal loop through the heart. This loop is called "a jumper," and it allows the heart to sit flat when worn as a pendant. Use the blue cord to wear the heart as a necklace and keep it in place over your throat chakra. After you have tied the cord around your neck, say, "I have something important to say, and I assert my power to be heard saying it and to have this information cherished and protected as I cherish and protect it." Wear the pendant for at least three hours.

Devoke.

This spell will ensure that you find your authoritative voice and that people will understand your meaning beyond just hearing your words. Here's a tip: You may say something that seems small but that has huge significance. Saying "I do" at a wedding is a common example of two small words that carry a big responsibility when spoken in the context of a relationship between two people who love each other.

Magickal Wisdom: You have an infinite capacity for love. The more love you give, the more you are able to receive. The reverse is true as well. The more love you accept, the more love you are capable of giving. Some people try to save up their love for one special person or reserve love only for romantic relationships. But love is broader than that. Expressions of love vary by relationship, as love between family members is different from love between friends or a romantic couple, but all these relationships share a bond of love. It is an honor to give and receive love, and love itself is a powerful force in the magickal realms.

Spell 48: Against Jealousy

YOU WILL NEED:

green modeling clay

Nothing can ply apart a friendship like jealousy. As you prepare for this spell, think about what it is that has made you jealous. At first it may seem to be everything about your friend is better. Think about it hard though. Break it down. Is it his or her clothes? Is it that he or she is the star of a team? Is it his or her grades? Is it his or her girlfriend or boyfriend? Is it his or her hair? Figure out what you wish you had. If you're having trouble, one way to start is to figure out what you're not jealous about. This will narrow down your list.

Part of this process is to help you identify what you do not envy about your friend. That's important because it reflects the balance in your friend's life. Think also about the aspects of your life that you do like. Maybe you can only think of one or two at first, but there has to be something about yourself that you like. This will be a jealousy counterbalance for you.

Also as preparation, give some thought to the kind of bug you dislike the most. Butterflies and ladybugs that are somewhat pretty and nice are not so good for this spell. Pick a nasty, unpleasant bug. Okay, all bugs are useful in nature, including dung beetles, which act as nature's janitors. But that doesn't mean you have to feel warm and cuddly about them. My theory is that there is a place in the world for all creatures, and the place for bugs is not next to me. So choose a bug that is gross (ticks, cockroaches), dirty (flies, worms), slimy (slugs, spit bugs), or annoying (hornets, yellow jackets). For me this is the mosquito, my all-time least favorite pest.

In finding the clay that you need, think about the feel of the material in your hands. What kind of clay do you like to handle? There are many kinds including baker's dough or modeling clay. Keep in mind that you will throw away what you make when you are done.

Keep the truth firmly in mind: grass is grass, and it is the same under your feet or someone else's.

The Spell: Ground and center. Cast the circle.

Stand tall with your arms at your sides. Raise your hands keeping them straight, and as you do, raise energy from the ground. Visualize that energy is lifting up in streams from your fingers and filling you and, especially, your hands.

Take out your clay. Say, "Unformed substance of the earth, I fill you with energy." And start to work the clay in your hands. At first don't make a shape. Start out by kneading and palming it to get it warm and full of your energy. Roll it into a cylinder, fold it, and do it again. When you've worked with it enough to get it the same temperature as your hands, separate the clay into three equal-size pieces. Take one of those pieces and start forming the type of bug you chose as your least favorite. As you do, think about how you like to keep your distance from this bug, how little you like seeing it, and how disgusting it would be to touch a real one. Mold the clay with your hands to be the best replica of this bug as you can. It doesn't have to be exact, but try hard to get it as accurate as you can.

Remember, the point of this isn't to prove that you're an artist; it's to get your energy about this bug in that clay. When you're done with all three, set them in front of you. Use your athame to point at them, and say, "Clay, I gave you form and energy. I created three (name of bugs), and each one embodies the unpleasantness of the original. And despite how dislikable these bugs are, jealousy is even worse. I charge you (bugs) with harboring jealousy inside you."

Then put the clay bugs on the ground. Take the palm of your hand and squash one flat. Say, "Jealousy, be gone with this bug!" Use your foot to stomp on the second one. Say, "Jealousy, your days are over!" You can either squash or stomp the third one, or you can sit on it to smash it with your butt. Say, "Jealousy, disappear and never bother me again."

Devoke.

Later take the smashed bugs outside and throw them away never to be seen again.

Magickal Wisdom: Plan destructive spells carefully.

If the action you intend to perform in your spell is destructive, choose carefully when deciding which items you want to accompany these actions. Clay is perfect for this spell against jealousy because pounding it doesn't hurt it. It changes shape as it is meant to do, and your energy returns to the earth because clay is merely a form of earth. It's a visceral way of getting rid of the negativity you've built up inside yourself. You can also cut string, rip paper, and throw plates to shatter them.

Taking something that has naturally come from a plant or animal means that you have the blessing of that plant or animal's spirit. You do not have that blessing if you kill the plant or animal. You can take something from the plant or animal without killing it. For example, you can take a flower or leaf off a plant and you can take some fur shed from a dog or a cat claw that has come off in a scratch box, and you have still left both the plant and the animal thriving. There is a difference between using something from a plant or animal and taking away its life.

Spell 49: For Strength in Your Decisions and Actions

YOU WILL NEED:

piece of tree bark

permanent marker

At some point in your life, you'll need to stand up for one of your opinions by taking action. This is one of the most important spells in this book because figuring out who you are and what path you as an individual will choose will lead to fulfillment. People who don't do this regret it later in life. They tend to feel that they never followed their dreams. And standing up to do something you want or believe starts the conscious act of choosing what you need to do to fulfill your calling.

As you prepare for this spell, think about what matters to you. You are an expert in who you are, and what is right for you. Throughout life, people will try to convince you about what to think or do, from friends with their own opinions to television advertisements. You can express your opinions, but not everyone listening might be in the frame of mind to understand you or to honor your opinions and to accept how you choose to act on them. While it is always good to listen to other opinions with an open mind, you are going to make up your own mind.

Once you've formed an opinion about something important to you, you may decide to take action, and you have got to have the strength to stand up for yourself. Concentrate on the strong spine you need if you are forced to confront anyone about your actions.

Oak is a very good tree for this spell because it represents strength. Birch is good because the bark curls and protects. But any tree bark that feels right to you is fine. You know the drill about asking permission first. It's better to take a piece of bark that has already fallen from a tree, but it's okay to take a small amount of bark from a living tree if it's already peeling off and won't hurt the tree.

The Spell: Ground and center. Cast the circle.

Stand tall, and press the bark on the top of your head. This is where your crown chakra is located, the energy center associated with your higher being and spiritual purpose in life. Visualize that disk opening on the top of your skull, and visualize the bark becoming one with that energy, your spiritual power center.

Say, "Bark, you came from a tree, and while attached you protected that tree. Now it is time to protect me. Help me to stand tall and firm like the tree."

Then sit down and feel the inside of the bark. All bark has a smooth side that was on the inside. This is part of why bark is perfect for this spell. The outside is the tough, protective layer, which represents your straight spine that stands up for who you are and what you believe. But the inside of the bark is melded perfectly to the tree's core, which represents your personality and inner decisions. Draw this rune: ↑ , as it is associated with the bright star that points the way, the proper direction. If that for some reason doesn't resonate for you, you can also draw a compass, as this is also a symbol for direction: ◌

The next step may seem funny, but it's important. Tell the bark one opinion of yours that you would stick to even if someone gave you a hard time about it. Here's the thing. You have to say it aloud. Go on, "I believe that . . ." or "(Here state your opinion) is important to me." Tell the bark that you're counting on it to stand up for this opinion and recognize its importance. Make a firm statement of this as you're saying it, just as if you were saying something important to an audience. You can make this statement even stronger by saying what you're going to do about that opinion. For example, "I've decided that I'm going to recycle whenever I can because this is good for the earth, so whenever anyone says it's okay to throw away a can or bottle, I'm going to insist that I carry it to a recycling bin."

Keep this special bark on your altar with the writing facing down so that it's hidden. Whenever you have an opinion that's important to you, go ahead and tell the bark.

Devoke.

Magickal Wisdom: Figure out who you are and stand for it spiritually.

Do you remember the Wiccan Rede from the spell for protection in the cafeteria? "Do what you will" is the second half of it. This means that your path of action must be guided by what you want for your life. You fill every day with the small choices you make. Some of these lead to bigger decisions. Some of your actions based on your decisions will lead others to judge you. Here's an example. One small decision, "Should I eat a baloney sandwich?" may lead to a larger question, "Should I become a vegetarian?" If you were to become a vegetarian, your parents might, for example, decide that you have become a rebellious teen because it may mean that you need special meals when the rest of the family is eating chicken for dinner. But your friends might think that you are cool. As you sort through the good and bad reasons for doing anything, keep in mind that you do not need anyone else's acceptance, however nice it is to have others respect your opinion. Working with magick will naturally lead you to pursue your goals and dreams. And many would say that your path, or purpose in life, is magickal in itself, even though day by day it may not seem that way.

Spell 50: Against Gossip

YOU WILL NEED:

> paper
> black pen
> red pen

Gossip travels faster than the speed of light, and people make up their minds based on thirdhand knowledge. Even if the gossip involves you but isn't primarily about you, it's disturbing. It can be a real pain to deal with a rumor about you or about someone else. As you prepare for this spell, think about what's circulating that you don't like. It's spoken or written misinformation being spread (e-mail counts as writing). It's "loud" now, and by that I mean that it's circulating and coming back to you as if it were important and true information. But it's not. And you know that. Think about how to turn down the volume. You can do this with your voice by lowering your tone and speaking softly.

The Spell: Ground and center. Cast the circle.

Sit in the center. Face north and connect to the ability that cold has to stop something. North is associated with winter, snow, and ice. Frost kills living plants. That's exactly what you want to have happen to gossip. When you've connected with this visualization, pick up the black pen and write all but the last line of the incantation:

> He said
> She said
> We said
> They said
> You said
> I said
> Whispers gone

Use the red pen to write the last line, "whispers gone." Annunciate each word as you read through this incantation three times. Start by saying the first two lines of the spell loudly and firmly: "He said, she said." Gradually let your voice get softer throughout the spell until you whisper it the third time through. The third and final time you say the last four words, "I said whispers gone," and use a strong, definite tone of voice. In doing so, you are sending your energy out into the world to carry forth your request.

Then rip up the paper with the incantation written on it into many tiny pieces. While standing, hold out your arms and sprinkle the papers to the floor. Watch them fall like silent snow onto the ground.

Devoke, and make a slapping noise as you dust your already clean hands. (This is the gesture for "I'm done with that and good riddance!")

If someone confronts you about the gossip, tell them you don't know anything about it and don't care to hear it. The best way to stop gossip is not to continue it. That's both practical and magickal advice.

Magickal Wisdom: Avoid baneful and brat magick.

Do not use baneful magick—magick meant to hurt someone else—or brat magick—magick meant to cause mischief to someone else or just to be pesky. Many people like the idea of getting revenge upon someone by casting a spell to cause him or her physical or emotional pain. At some point, everyone gets angry with someone else for something he or she did, but it's not appropriate to turn to magick when you feel that way. I bring this up in connection with this spell against gossip because it's tempting to want to get back at the person who's causing you grief and anxiety. I'll remind you about the other magickal wisdom sections that say that you should never cause harm to anyone even unintentionally and that what you send out into the world comes back to you magnified by three. Do you really want the bad karma associated with casting a baneful spell? Do you really want something three times worse than what you send out to come back to you? (I might add that it tends to come back when you least want it, when you're already trying to get through something else that's difficult.) There is always a way to cast a spell without affecting someone else. At the very least you can cast a spell to protect yourself.

Spell 51: For Helping a Friend

YOU WILL NEED:

photograph or image of yourself
penny
glue
piece of candy

This is a tricky spell because it is a selfless act on your part, and you have to listen carefully to what your friend is saying so that you're focusing your energy where your friend wants it. You also have to use your best judgment because your friend may want you to do something that you know is against the magickal ethics you've learned, and in that case, you have to explain gently that it's going to be worse in the end if you perform that type of magick for him or her. Say you have an idea and describe this spell, or better yet, have your friend read it.

When you do this spell, it's probably going to be your

friend's first magickal experience. She may not have ever been in a circle. Before you start, explain what you want to do. It's a good idea to have her read the spell ahead of time just like you do as part of your preparation. Ask her if she's comfortable with this, and give her room to say no, she'd rather hang out and listen to your favorite CD together. Don't force anyone to do magick. If she agrees to go ahead and wants to do the spell, tell her that at the beginning of the spell she'll have to say aloud that she wants to be there doing that.

As you look for the photograph of yourself, realize that you are not going to get this picture back, so you may want to make a color photocopy or you may want to create a drawing of yourself. Ask your friend if she wants to be in the drawing or photograph too, and find a photograph of both of you or make one. If you make a drawing, remember that stick figures are fine. Try to put some identifying traits in the picture such as eye color and hairstyle. Since you also need a piece of candy, I suggest a hard candy such as a peppermint.

The Spell: Ground and center. Do this aloud so that your friend can also do it. Go slowly so that she can keep up. Remember that you've practiced this many times, but she hasn't. Cast the circle. Tell her what you're doing aloud as you do it. Call the quarters aloud. Offer to let your friend do it with you.

Next, you need to pose a challenge to your friend so that she agrees to be there and commits to doing the spell with you. Ask her, "Are you in this sacred circle with the good intention of doing magick?" and wait for her answer. Then ask her, "Are you ready to cast this spell with me?" and wait for her answer. If either answer is no, devoke and stop the process. If yes to both, go on. It may seem silly, but it is a way of getting the other person's explicit approval and participation, especially if he or she was quiet during the circle-casting process.

Take out your photograph or drawing of yourself. Show it to your friend, and say, "Here is my image. I add luck to it by binding this penny to it." Glue the penny on the back of the photograph or drawing. Then say, "Tell me what difficulty you are about to confront," and wait for her to tell you.

Then say, "I give this photograph to you to take with you during the difficulty you must confront. Keep it with you, and it will give you luck and power as if I were with you myself."

Then take out the candy and put it on your altar. Hold your athame pointing on it, and say, "Peppermint, I charge you with calming, healing powers." Give it to your friend, and tell her to eat it after she's done with what she's about to do as a calming, healing reward for being done.

Devoke, and both clap your hands in unison.

Tell your friend shortly after the spell is over that either your friend should return the photograph and penny to you so that you can take them apart or that your friend should enlist to do this. Take the penny outside and put it in the earth as thanks for using the energy.

Magickal Wisdom: Be a giver as well as a taker.

When you borrow earth energy, you need to give it back. Many times you'll bring energy up from the earth during a spell. Sometimes you'll bring it down from the sky. Whatever excess energy you don't use needs to be returned. And you'll find that it flows to you better if you return energy later after you've finished with it. Tell your friend to take apart the talisman and release it once the magick is done or the spell will backfire. Even if the magick has happened, the energy needs to be freed so that the positive result of the magick stays with your friend.

Spell 52: For Staying Connected to a Friend While You Are Apart

YOU WILL NEED:

   3 cords each 3 feet long: one in your favorite color,
      one in your friend's favorite color, and one white
   some scented oil

Many times life circumstances pull apart people who are meant to be together. Concentrate on remaining close and preserving your special bond no matter what the reason for your separation.

As you prepare for this spell, remember that you both have to want to do this. You are doing an act together. You are bringing your friend into sacred space to do it. Ask directly if your friend wants to do this spell. Be open to the answer no if that's what it truly is. If you both really want to do this spell, then talk about your favorite colors. Each of you should be able to choose a favorite color and answer a few questions about it: What is your favorite color? Why? What does it remind you of? Then get the cords in the colors you need.

You are about to make an umbilical cord that connects you to the other person. You must absolutely trust this person completely. If either one of you decides that the cords should be unbraided, then you must both agree that you will do it.

The oil should have a nice smell. You can make some by adding a drop of vanilla, peppermint extract, or another herbal essence to a small amount of vegetable oil.

The Spell: Lead your friend through the grounding and centering process. Cast the circle aloud and allow your friend to cast it with you if desired. Call the quarters for your friend to hear and join in if desired. This will help you both to be between the worlds together.

Once in sacred space, ask your friend two questions: "Do you come to this circle of your own free will?" "Are you ready to craft a magickal bond together?" Take some oil and rub a small amount on the middle of your friend's forehead. Have your friend do the same to you.

Sit together across from each other. Put some peppercorns in your hands and shake them as if they're a rattle. Then hand them to your friend to do the same. Say, "These peppercorns heighten our sense of touch so that we feel our connection even when we're apart." Take three deep breaths, and say, "We are going to braid two cords so that we can each keep one with us while we're apart. These will be our umbilical cords to each other, our direct links to know that in spirit we're together even if our bodies are far apart." Cut each of the three cords in half so that there are two sets.

Take three cords, one in your favorite color, one in your friend's favorite color, and one white, and make a knot at one end of that first set of three. One of you should hold the three cords together at the end while the other begins to braid them. While braiding, say all the things aloud about the other person that are positive and good attributes of that person and of your mutual friendship. When the cord is half braided, switch sides. Hold the cord while your friend braids the rest, all the while saying what she thinks are the best things about you and your friendship. The person who did not make the first knot should be the one to tie the knot at the other end. Repeat this process with the other set of three cords.

When you're done with both cords, you should each hold one braid. One at a time, give the cord to the other person saying "Our lives intertwine like a braid. Our relationship is secure like a pair of knots. With this cord know that I am always with you when you need me." Then together, say, "These braids are our umbilical cords to each other when we cannot be together in person, these cords connect us in spirit."

Next, you must each promise aloud to undo the cord if one of you wants that. Say, "I give this cord to you as a gift, but it is also a responsibility. I promise you that I will untie this cord and release its power should you ask me to. I hope you will tell me why, but I will not require you to do so before undoing it." Then together say, "So mote it be."

Devoke. Both clap your hands and stomp your feet at the same time but not in unison. This makes a sound like a herd of elephants, and there is no stopping that.

Magickal Wisdom: Magick does not know distance.

Magickally there is no distance between you and someone you love, even if you're physically far apart. You know that the web of energy connects all things and that this is how your spell causes change once you cast it. It takes time for changes to happen. But a magickal connection to someone else doesn't need this time. With the magickal connection, energy doesn't travel at the speed of sound or light. It's there instantaneously. This spell honors the love you have with your friend. It doesn't have to be romantic love, but it could be. The cord reminds you that while your friend may be physically distant, the love you share is always close. I have found that this cord spell works even after one of the two people dies.

Spell 53: For Sealing True Friendship

YOU WILL NEED:

    1 white candle

    2 candles in your favorite colors

    couple of different sheets of paper

scissors

pen

aluminum foil

a few drops of scented oil

Every once in a while you have a friendship so deep that you want to seal that bond with a ritual. This spell is meant to honor a deep relationship. Make sure you have a history of regular, everyday time together before you cast this spell together.

Traditionally, this spell was a ritual to honor "blood brothers." But do not get out a knife and expect to cut yourself so that you and your friend can mix your blood together. That could be dangerous. (What if you cut yourself too deeply? What if one of you unknowingly has a disease?) Blood brothers does not mean that people used to mix their blood. It means that the friendship was so strong that one friend would spill his own blood to defend and protect the other if necessary. It refers to the feeling behind the bond, not what the friends did to seal their friendship.

You and your friend should prepare for this spell together. Have your friend read it over so that you can each be focusing your minds on the spell you're going to do together. Think about this special person in your life. Think about what you've been through together. Think about what you share. Think about how you're similar. Think about how you're different and complement each other because of your differences. Think about what it means to give someone a gift that is a part of you and to seal it shut so that you can't take back your gift. Think about what it means to receive the same from someone else.

The one white candle should be a long, thin taper. The other two candles don't need to be large. Your candle should feel good in your hand. Help your friend do the same. Handmade paper with flowers in it is great for this spell, but any paper will do.

The Spell: Ground and center. Cast the circle going through this process aloud to help your friend. Give your friend enough time to ground and center because your friend probably is not as practiced at this as you are. Encourage your friend to help cast the circle and call the quarters if so desired.

When the circle is cast, turn and look at your friend eye to eye. Say to your friend, "We are between the worlds. Do you come to this circle freely for the purpose of working magick?" Wait for your friend to answer. If you receive a positive response, anoint your friend with oil on the forehead and have your friend do the same to you. Then say, "Do you realize that once cast, the spell can be broken, but we can never go back to the time before it was cast?"

Sit down facing each other. Hold hands and make a long, low "ahhhhhh" sound together. Visualize energy flowing clockwise from your right hand into your friend's left hand and from your friend's right hand into your left hand. Do this for a few minutes until you both feel in harmony with each other.

Take the flower paper and cut out a square about 7 inches long on each side. Take another piece of paper, and cut it into a circle about 3 inches in diameter. Write "friend" on it and decorate it. Put your paper circle in the center of the paper square and fold the four corners of the square so that they meet and cover the circle. In essence, you've just made an envelope for the circle. Then put the aluminum foil down and put the square on it. Drip wax from your candle (the one that's your favorite color) over the place where the square's four corners meet. Press your thumb into the wax to seal the envelope shut. Your friend should also make an envelope but seal it with wax from the other candle, the one your friend chose.

When you are both done, stand up and put your envelopes over your solar plexuses, the hollow between your belly button and the bottom of your ribs. This is your third chakra, the energy center associated with understanding and the wide range of emotions. While holding your envelopes pressed with both hands over your belly buttons, both of you then make the long, low, "ahhhhhhh," sound again.

Last, give your envelope to your friend. Take some time to say why you're giving this gift, the envelope sealed with a part of yourself in it. Then have your friend give you the other envelope and also say why.

When you're done, both devoke together. Both stomp your feet to ground out the excess energy. By lifting your knees high as if you were parading, you'll reinforce your togetherness even after the spell ends.

Magickal Wisdom: Honor the magickal within the mundane.

Profound mundane experiences can transcend the ordinary to become magickal. Knowing when to cast this spell is the trickiest part about it. How will you know when it's the right time for you both? How will you know if the connection is deep enough between the two of you? I find that something happens in which one of you stands up for the other one or helps the other one in such a way that you know nobody else would have done that. Or you both go through a traumatic experience together. And when that happens, you may want to honor that friend, to acknowledge the unspoken commitment that you've made to each other. If your friendship is truly deep enough, every spirit around you will know that you've a bond on a spiritual level, and you'll not need to do this spell. But casting this spell shows each other that you acknowledge and accept this bond and that you each intend to honor it as long as you live. The unspoken bond becomes enhanced by magick when it is recognized for what it is.

Adeptitude

In this chapter of spells about friends, you have stepped over the threshold of simple spells to complex magick. That's because these spells don't just call an item to you. They change situations in both tenor and outcome. You're gently asking that the universe surround you with the spirit of positive energy without forcing anything on anyone else.

Bringing more friendship into your life and sharing your hopes and dreams with someone will enhance your ability to direct change in the web of energy. When you care about someone, you're more vulnerable when he or she is hurt or angry, but your joy in connecting with them far outweighs that risk and upholds the most basic law of magick. Laws are serious, and you may wonder how all of this relates to the most important law of magick. Love is the law. When you act with pure love in your heart, your magick resonates with the entire web of energy throughout the world, and you've the greatest chance of lasting change. It will vibrate throughout you, and if you pay close attention, you'll notice a tingling sensation and calmness when you've the resolve of love at heart.

What is the greatest law of magick?

Love. **Love is the greatest law of magick.**

By now you see the world in a magickal way, and you're able to cast spells that interact with objects, your environment, around other people, and with people who want to join you. You're ready to initiate deep spellcraft on yourself to start the most intimate work of magick in connecting with love in other people. And now that you know that the greatest law of magick is love, you'll understand why the ultimate chapter in this book is about dating, relationships, and love. In the proceeding pages you'll learn the answer to the question: What is the key to leading a magickal life? Move forward to become the enchanter you have always been meant to be.

CHAPTER 7

THE ENCHANTER: SPELLS ABOUT DATING AND LOVE

FINALLY, HERE WE ARE at the chapter that most people want to skip to from the beginning. Who hasn't wanted to cook up a little love potion to catch a romantic partner who's the stuff of dreams? We all have wanted that, and in this chapter you'll find a spell to call for a date, for a steady relationship, and ultimately your true love. Of course, you'll know already that you can't have a specific person in mind or make someone buckle to your every desire. Slavery was abolished a long time ago and with good reason. But it seems to me that you're even more powerful when you attract people to you and have them stay because they want to be with you rather than because you've forced them to do so.

You're better off if a boyfriend or girlfriend starts as a friend first because that sets the emotional foundation of lasting partnerships. Romantic relationships can become intense because you may share a level of physical intimacy that goes beyond that of friends. Once you do that, it's hard to go back to just friends. But the love I'm talking about in this chapter isn't focused on holding hands, kissing, or sex. Sex is short and easy. I'm focusing on the deep feelings of having a loving relationship which is much more difficult to keep going in a loving, respectful way than kisses.

If you've been going slowly and casting at least three to five spells per chapter, you've probably undergone a lot of personal growth. Certainly, your magickal skill has improved whether or not you've noticed it. Take some time as you prepare to cast these spells to think about who you are, what you want in life, and where you're going. You don't have to have all the answers up front, but if you keep thinking about who you are, how you're changing, and what your dreams are, you'll be in a lot better position to achieve them. Your magickal book of shadows will help with this process a great deal, so it's a good idea to keep up with that. Spells about love invigorate that primal center in each of us. People are meant to feel attraction and close connection with romantic partners. In other words, these spells about love most likely relate to your primary spiritual path.

Every time you cast a spell, you're moving energy. And love is one of the primary forces of energy. Ideally, love should be the motivation behind every spell you cast. I'll admit that not every spell seems like it has much to do with love. This chapter has a couple of spells to get new clothes, and while an outfit will make you look good and might get you a hot date, it's not the same as working magick to find the partner of your dreams. But it does keep up your self-confidence and self-image, and these too are important and should have love at their core. May you have many nights kissing under the stars after casting these spells.

Here is your grounding and centering meditation for the spells in this chapter. It's based on water, which by now you know is associated with west, emotions, and wisdom. All of these are fine qualities to keep in mind while dating, falling in love, and other matters of the heart.

Grounding and Centering Meditation: Water

Take a deep breath and feel your heart. As you let the breath out, feel the fuzziness around its edges and the warmth of it.

Take another deep breath and let it out slowly, all the while keeping in touch with your heart. Imagine liquid in your heart pulsing up and out of you.

Now imagine that liquid is a tiny spring of water on top of a mountain. With force it erupts out of the ground and flows in a tiny stream down the mountain. It continues as a brook at the bottom passing over land and rocks where it gushes as a waterfall.

Imagine the water flowing into a river with gentle, easy curves and a lazy pace.

Then imagine the slow river emptying into the ocean where waves unfurl onto the beach and then draw back in a continuous motion. Feel this continuous

motion in your own heart. And when you feel
ready, proceed to casting the circle.

Here is how to cast the circle for the spells in this chapter. This is a much different way to cast a circle than in
prior chapters. You are not calling to quarters as you have
in every chapter previously, you're invoking the quarters
and the Sky, Earth, and Center. This is an advanced
method of casting a circle because you are drawing the
quarters to the circle with a focused energy and then you
concentrate on calling to the forces Above, Below, and
Center. It emphasizes that you hope to walk the path on
the earth in a centered, balanced way so that you live your
life with the purpose of the spirit world.

Circle Casting: As Above, So Below

Stand in the center of your circle. Point your athame
to the north, and visualize sparks and energy
spurting forth.

Shoot the sparking energy from the north to the east,
from the east to the south, from the south to the
west, and from the west to the north to complete
the circle.

Now visualize a second ring going clockwise in the
same place the first ring was but replenishing it
with a stronger band of energy.

Now visualize a third ring, the strongest yet, zooming around the circle to add to the first two.

Put your athame back on your altar, and pick up your wand. Stand in the center, and say:

East, South, West, North, I call the circle round.

Again I say, East, South, West, North, I call the circle round.

Three times makes it hold fast, East, South, West, North, I call the circle round.

Reach above your head holding your wand at one end with the other end pointed up, and say, "Sky, you protect and cover me."

Reach down to the floor and touch it with your wand, and say "Earth, you support and nurture me."

Stand still in the center of your circle again, and hold your wand close to your chest, and say, "Center, you balance and stabilize me." Say, "As above, so below; as without, so within. I am between the worlds." Now you are ready to begin.

The Spells

Spell 54: For Finding the Right Outfit

YOU WILL NEED:

2 different sizes and pieces of fabric

piece of trim or lace

button

small bit of ribbon
flower petals
needle
light yellow thread

As you prepare for this spell, think about how you want to look. Do you see yourself with your hair up or loose and flowing? Do you see yourself with a long flowing dress or hip-hugging jeans? Do you have a particular color in mind? Imagine how you would look wearing this outfit and think of how you will feel. Once you've done that, toss out the image of what you will look like because you need to be open to the outfit you find. The clothes may have elements of what you have envisioned but may not be the same as what you see in your mind. And you have to be open to an outfit that is unexpected at least in some ways. What you want to keep in focus is the feeling you want while wearing it.

You should like the color, look, and feel of all the materials you are using for this spell: the fabric, trim or lace, and button. The two pieces of fabric should be different from each other, and one should be bigger than the other is. I like to do this with two circles to remind me of the circle that I cast, but other shapes work too. You should also like the flower, and preferably dry it yourself. (If you'd prefer leaves to flowers, as many guys do, try to pick unusual shaped leaves or ones with multicolored patterns.) The best way to dry it is in the sunlight, for example, on a windowsill, but in a pinch you can heat it briefly in the oven. Don't worry about matching the fabric, trim, and button with each other.

The Spell: Ground and center. Cast the circle.

Sit calmly in the center of the circle, and think to yourself about being calm and being centered in yourself and being in the center of the circle. And then think about how you are in the center of your world, not in a bad, self-centered way, but in a balanced, everything-around-me-supports-me way. Then think about how there is an outfit in the world for you that is perfect for this occasion. Visualize how you will feel wearing it. Take the larger piece of fabric and put it on the floor. Put the palm of your hands down onto it and visualize that feeling flowing down your arms and out your hands into the fabric.

Take up your light yellow thread and needle. Look at the yellow thread and think how the yellow reminds you of the first sunlight of the morning filtering through the trees. Thinking about the color yellow and dawn will connect you to East so that you are inspired in finding the right outfit. Sew the smaller piece of fabric to the other as a patch, but don't close it entirely. The stitches don't need to be really neat or tight; they just need to keep the smaller piece of fabric on the larger one. Then stuff the dried flower petals inside the pouch you've just created between the two pieces of fabric and finish sewing the smaller one to the larger one so that the petals can't fall out. Sew the lace onto the larger piece of fabric to decorate it. Sew the button on wherever you like as a decoration. As you're doing this, keep thinking about how you will adorn yourself to be beautiful. Fold the ribbon and sew the ends to the circle making a loop so that you can hang this charm. When you're finished sewing it, hold it above your head, and say, "Simple fabric, trim, button, and ribbon, alone you're nothing, but I bound you together to call my outfit to me. May it be beautiful and perfect and fit me just right. So mote it be."

Devoke.

Hang it on a hanger in your closet, and leave it there until you find your clothes. It's holding a place in your closet for the real outfit. When you get it, put it in your closet where you hung this magickal ornament. Remove the ornament, cut the thread that sewed it together, cut the fabric and lace, and throw the pieces away.

Magickal Wisdom: Personal investment makes someone most qualified to cast a spell.

Magick works best when done by the one wanting the results. Getting someone else to do spells for you diminishes the impact of your own will, and your will is a key part of the spell. You have the power of your desire. Nobody else desires what you want more than you do. The corollary to this is that if others want something, the spell will work better if they do it themselves. If close friends know that you've been casting some spells, you may be asked to work some magick for them. Magick can work for someone else, but it's a lot more effective if the individual does it. Your answer to a friend could be, "I could do it, but, you know, there is somebody other than me who would be better and more powerful for this spell. And that is you because you are the one who wants this the most."

Spell 55: For Receiving a Passionate Kiss

YOU WILL NEED:

chocolate kiss

5 blackberries

plate with a rim

napkin

pinch of nutmeg

A kiss is a symbol of love, a moment of connecting, and it can temporarily blend your spirit with someone else's spirit. It is human nature to want a passionate kiss like a flower unfolding. A kiss can be a spark that starts a wonderful relationship or the culmination of a romantic good-bye.

As you prepare for this spell, think about what it means to be in the present moment. A kiss requires you to be 100 percent present. If your mind is off daydreaming about something else, you are going to miss your kiss, so be conscious of living in the here and now while doing this spell (really while doing any spell).

I like to get a bag of Hershey®'s Kisses to use for this spell, but any bite-size piece of pure chocolate (no nuts or rice) works. The chocolate should be a bit melted like warm butter so that it's not hard or crunchy if you bite into it. Look for ripe and juicy blackberries that have the deepest, richest juice. If you can't find juicy blackberries, substitute another juicy berry (not just another fruit, but specifically a berry). The plate is for catching juice, so a plate with a rim will be best.

The Spell: Ground and center. Cast the circle.

Sit in the center facing your altar with the chocolate in front of you. Put the chocolate on the plate in front of you. The chocolate should be bare, so if it has got a wrapper, take that off. Think about that melty chocolate and how pleasing it will be in your mouth.

As you are working this spell, visualize a little slow motion in it so that when you get this kiss, it too will be like the slow motion that happens when the world stops around you. As you picture the kiss you want, concentrate on having hypersensitivity so that you soak up the entire kiss feeling, every bit of it.

Take a berry and squeeze it over the chocolate so that the juice falls onto the chocolate. Do this with five berries in a row. (When you are done, use the napkin to wipe off your hands.) Then take a pinch of nutmeg and put some over the top of the chocolate so that it sticks in the berry juice. The nutmeg, which is associated with your sense of taste, will increase this sense when you're kissing.

Hold the plate with the berry-juice-dripped bite of chocolate, and say, "A kiss is a gift to receive and a gift to give. May a passionate kiss come to me. So mote it be."

Put the berry juice covered chocolate in your mouth and savor it as it melts in your mouth. Try not to chew it. Go ahead and lick the excess berry juice off the plate when you are done. Lick your lips.

Devoke.

Magickal Wisdom: A kiss blends magickal energy.

A kiss temporarily melds the magickal energy of two people. Ever wonder why people talk about a kiss as a magical moment? Or as electrifying? That is because a kiss is both of those things. Many people think of kissing as an earthy, lustful act, but in the path of natural magick, a kiss is a way of mixing two people's energy with each other. The energy that is raised and blended during a kiss is a sort of natural intensifier because one and one does not equal two, it equals a new being with a higher resonance for a short time.

Spell 56: For Becoming a Soulful Kisser

YOU WILL NEED:

white piece of paper

3 or more lipsticks in different colors

pen

several napkins

Some kisses are quick pecks on the cheek as if to say "thank you." Some are "air kisses" where you really just touch someone else's cheek and make a kissing sound without touching your lips to them. Often these are kisses to say "hello." A kiss on the forehead usually signifies nurturing love, the sort a parent gives a child. All of these are useful kisses. And the magick in them comes from the emotions behind them. But the kiss of lovers is a spark meant to stir the heart in the people touching.

As you prepare for this spell, think about the practical aspects of kissing. Think about the muscles that you use to kiss. Sure, you use your lips, but what about your eyes? During a kiss are your eyes open or closed? Do you do both for different types of kisses? What about your arms and hands? Do you embrace someone? During an air kiss, many people hold the person close but keep them from pressing against them. Do you keep your hands still, or do you caress the person while you are kissing? And equally important, take some time to focus on how you feel during a kiss. Are you aware only of yourself? What about the other person? What about your surroundings?

You need to fold the piece of paper in half, so it can't be cardboard thickness. Also, I recommend at least $8^{1}/_{2} \times 11$ inches (normal-sized paper) or larger. You'll need lots of lipsticks and lip glosses that smell good and have different colors. The more the better, but at least three. Go a little wild. If you're a guy, think about theater and try colors like orange, blue, or black. The napkins are to wipe your lips between colors if you want to. The previous color might get on the new color if you don't do this, but that's only a problem if you think it is or if you're going from a darker color to a lighter color.

The Spell: Ground and center. Cast the circle.

Start this spell by standing in the center and putting your fingers on your lips. Feel your lips with your fingertips. Visualize energy coming up from the earth, through the floor, into your feet, up your legs and torso, and out of your fingertips into your lips. Say, "Lips I charge you with energy to be passionate." When your lips feel warm and charged with energy, sit down.

Put your paper down horizontally so that it is wider than it is high. Fold your paper in half vertically so that it looks like you pulled a page from a book. Draw a butterfly shape so that the center of the page with the fold is the body of the butterfly and each folded half of the paper has top and bottom wings. If you're having trouble, think of making a letter B on the right-hand side and a reverse B on the left side. Your paper should look like this:

Now get out your lipsticks and lip gloss colors. Put them on one at a time and use your lips to kiss the paper. Make some kisses with your lips puckered. Make some with your lips open wide. Be creative and fill all the wings with lots of kiss marks on both the left and the right sides. You can enhance this spell by saying the color names aloud. They usually have fun names. And if you do not like the name of a color, make up a better one!

When you've filled the butterfly with kiss marks from your lips, fold the paper on the crease you made from folding it at the beginning of the spell. The butterfly should not be visible. Press the paper together, and rub it with the heel of your hand. Then open the butterfly and see how the colors mixed together and made a new design of kisses on both sets of wings.

Stand up holding your butterfly, and say, "Like the butterfly I transform. I impassion my lips so that I may become a soulful kisser with my whole body. So mote it be"

Devoke.

You can put the butterfly on your altar or on your wall if you think it won't attract people to ask what it is. You can say that it's a piece of art you made, but don't puncture your spell by telling people about the magick behind it.

Magickal Wisdom: Personal transformation is high magick.

You probably noticed that I didn't title this spell "For Getting a Soulful Kiss." This spell does not concentrate on just one kiss the way the previous spell does. This spell is about a higher, more potent type of magick. This spell has the power to change you as a person, and that is personal transformation which we call "high magick" as opposed to "low magick" which is about making mundane changes in life. High magick is the most important type of magick we have. If you do this spell once, you will become a better kisser. No doubt about it. But if you do this spell repeatedly over time and you focus on turning yourself into a soulful kisser and the gift you are giving with each kiss, you will gradually turn into someone who can give a kiss as an expression of your soul.

Spell 57: For Getting a Date

YOU WILL NEED:

piece of paper

envelope

blue ink

feather

The potential for romance sparks in spring blossoms, in sultry summer evenings, in the crisp fall air, and in the warm fireplace blazes of winter. Anytime is a good time for romance!

As you prepare for this spell, think about meeting someone or getting to know someone better. A date should be about having a good time without pressure. Concentrate on the type of date you are looking for, whether you just want the romantic fun of hanging out with someone or whether you have a particular occasion like a dance or your prom in mind. You are putting an invitation out to the world to have a fun time that could lead to a romantic relationship but does not have to. Try not to put pressure on it or load it with expectations.

The piece of paper doesn't need to be large, but you'll need to fold it once. Look around outside for a feather large enough to hold as a pen and with a stiff quill. You can get ink at any crafts store. You want an invitation to a date, so you're going to create an invitation to show the magickal world what you want.

The Spell: Ground and center. Cast the circle.

Hold your paper and fold it in half so that it's like a card. Focus your energy on what you want to say in your invitation. Concentrate on what you want to feel and happen during this date rather than what you want to result from this date once it's over. Think about paper as a thin layer of natural fibers and about how it can take your message and deliver it to the world.

Then hold the feather. Think of the feather as a symbol of East that corresponds to Air and communication. This is the perfect tool for conveying your desire. Hold the container of blue ink. Blue is the color associated with your throat chakra, and its color is blue. Thus, you are mixing the feather, the natural world's communication tool, with blue ink, a tool associated with your personal communication center, to increase your power of communicating to the universe that you want a date. In other words, you are coordinating different aspects of the spell to work together as a powerful combination.

The folded piece of paper will look like a note card or birthday card. On the front use the feather as a pen dipped in the ink to write "An invitation to a date" in decorative lettering. Then unfold the paper and write on the inside. Remember all those qualities you've been thinking about in preparation for this spell? Now's the time to write them on the inside. Be specific about how you want to feel during the date, and maybe about some of what you want to do, but do *not* write down someone else's name. It's fine to be brief since feather and ink aren't easy to use.

Go back to the front of the card. Next, you need to think carefully about the kind of connection you want to have with the person. What aspect of this person do you want the most? Do you want someone you can talk to? Do you want someone with a spiritual interest? Do you want a bowling partner? Think hard about this and draw a symbol that relates to what you want. If you want someone who listens well and responds attentively, consider drawing an ear to represent a good listener or a bird to represent a good communicator. If you want someone with a spiritual interest, consider drawing a spiral to symbolize a sacred path. If you want a bowling partner, consider drawing a bowling ball and pins. Remember that whatever quality you ask for will come through if your relationship with this person develops—do not expect it to manifest right away. You are asking for someone with this potential.

Finally, sign with only your first name. The magickal world will know who you are and nobody else needs to. This is for your own protection in case someone else inadvertently finds the card. Put your card in the envelope.

Sit in your circle facing your altar. Say, "Life is full of opportunities and invitations. I send this invitation out to open the opportunity for me to go on a date. I want to meet someone compatible with me and to have a fun time getting to know each other." Then put the card on your altar.

Devoke.

After you get the date, rip it up three times and bury the remnants.

Magickal Wisdom: Time is elastic.

Time is not the same in the spirit world as it is in the physical world. We experience time in a continuous linear way in which each minute passes with the same amount of time as every other minute. Our lives are filled with deadlines that press against us and with waiting that drives us to boredom. But the spirit world does not measure time this way. Time does not pass at the same rate in that world. Time matters less, which means a long time to us can be a mere blip in the spirit world. Keep this in mind and adjust your spell accordingly. You will need to allow some time for this spell to come true, but you probably want this date to happen sooner than next year. So you might want to give a month for it to happen. That sounds like a long time, and to you it is. But in the spirit world, it is not a long time. Be specific during your spell about the time frame you want by stating it aloud while you are in the circle.

Spell 58: For Attracting a Boyfriend

YOU WILL NEED:

paper that can be folded several times (tissue paper)
sharp scissors
pen

As you prepare for this spell, think of yourself. Are you ready for a relationship? You're not necessarily ready to settle down yet, but you're ready for a deeper connection than you get on a night out. A relationship is a way to know someone past the charming personality who entrances you on your first date. Why do you want a relationship? If it's to show off a hunk to your friends, that's not a great reason. If you're ready to put energy into a heart connection that involves giving and growing, then you're on the right track. Yeah, I figured you were, I just wanted to make sure because this spell isn't just about you—it'll call someone to you. While a relationship can bring security and stability, it also takes work because it exposes each of you to your less favorable sides because everyone has faults. Getting a boyfriend brings both the responsibility of working through problems and the yielding of great rewards of commitment and shared experiences.

Get very thin paper because you're going to fold the paper as many times as possible and then cut it. Tissue paper works well for this. Make sure you've got good, sharp scissors. As I say, you're going to be cutting through paper that's folded several times, and dull scissors are a drag for cutting through multiple layers of paper.

The Spell: Ground and center. Cast the circle.

Sit down in a cross-legged position. Put the back of your hands on your knees so that your palms and fingers are pointing up. Take a deep breath and let it out. Connect for a moment with your heart center.

Keep your piece of paper in your hand, and hum a low, solid tone, holding it as long as you can. Concentrate on the love you want to call to you, and fold your paper in half once. Concentrate on the fun, support, and nurturing you want to give and receive in this new relationship, and hold a hum in a higher tone than the one you used at first. Fold your paper in half again. Then say, "I want a boyfriend. I call an ongoing, romantic relationship to me. I am open to the right person coming along whomever that may be for the greater good of all." (Yes, that means you cannot have a specific guy in mind!) Then hold a higher tone and hum while you fold the paper in half again. You might want to stop at three folds because you'll have more control making the cuts. If you want to keep folding, continue humming higher each time you fold the paper in half again and say the incantation. If you make five folds it's possible but hard to cut through even with sharp scissors. The original size of the unfolded paper doesn't matter. You'll not be able to fold any sized paper more than six or seven times.

Then pick up your sharp scissors, and begin cutting shapes into the folded paper. Triangles are the easiest to make, but you're welcome to make any shapes you like. It's nice to put a circle somewhere by cutting a quarter of a circle on a corner. If you have an exacto knife, you can cut in the center of the paper rather than from the edge. As you make the cuts, focus your mind on how you want to feel in the relationship.

When you've finished making the cuts, unfold the paper to see the snowflake design that you created. Use your pen to write down three or more feelings you want during your new relationship. You might write things like *love, happiness, fun, honesty,* and *affection.* Say, "Every snowflake is individual. Bring me the individual who will be best for me. Let our love unfold together. So mote it be."

Devoke.

Tape this snowflake to your window at sunset so that the words you wrote on it face out. Leave it overnight to face the moon.

Magickal Wisdom: Love rewards those who can stand alone before those who cannot.

The magickal world honors those who are independent and confident on their own with love before those who are dependent and insecure. This is because someone who is able to be stable alone has matured enough to be ready for a soul mate more than someone who leans on a partner in a needy way does. If you're looking for a boyfriend but are having trouble finding one, perhaps it's because you haven't prepared for it with enough spiritual growth first. Take a step back and try to be independent for a while. Women tend to give lots of love and support even at their own expense. So it may seem strange that a woman who gives and gives won't be as attractive to a man as a woman who doesn't need to be in a relationship but knows her own limits. Unfortunately, some people feel helpless without being in a relationship. Not until one has grown enough not to need a partner is one actually ready for that partner. And this is when the magickal world will lead Mr. Right straight to you.

Spell 59: For Attracting a Girlfriend

YOU WILL NEED:

   2 red candles (preferably attached by the wick)
   matches
   your hair
   thin wire

A young woman's love, day in and out, can keep a guy going. But it's not easy to find the right gal. You're not going to find a lasting relationship with someone who's not suitable to your personality no matter how hard you try. You can attract her attention with flowers or a date, but you'll have to do more to convince her to stay with you, so this spell focuses on accepting your emotions and communicating them to a potential partner. It is strong magick day after day to maintain her happiness so that she stays with you willingly.

As you prepare for this spell, start by thinking of the obvious mundane things you do every day to keep up your appearance. You shower every day, change your athletic socks after practice, and comb your hair regularly. Unless you have a beard, you shave and probably most girls don't appreciate that enough. And why is it that so many guys put off cutting their toenails? Then think about the emotional reasons that you want a relationship. Think of the qualities that you want to draw to you. You want someone pretty, fun, supportive, and self-sufficient. (Why is it that so many girls need to be reassured that they're not fat?) You want someone who understands your inner being and what's important to you. I'm probably missing a whole lot of important qualities. These are just to get you going on the thought process. What's not okay is to have a particular person in mind.

The best candles for this spell are made with one common wick so they're still attached when you buy them. These can be found at most candle shops, but if you can't find them, two of the same kind of candles will do. The wire must be thin so that you can bend it. I recommend copper because it's a natural conduit for energy. You will need some of your hair. Don't hurt yourself by pulling out your hair, but don't use scissors to cut it. You want whole hairs, even though they're likely to be short. Use your comb or brush to remove hair gently that is ready to be pulled out. If you're bald, which enhances the masculine look by making a guy look distinguished, this spell also works with underarm hair.

The Spell: Ground and center. Cast the circle.

Take the piece of wire and coil it in a small circle around one of the two candles. If you don't have wire cutters, wrap the wire several times until it is all coiled. As you wrap the coil around the candle, say, "I give my love a circle of emotion for protection." In saying this, you are charging the candle to be both the person whom you are attracting to you as well as the love that you feel toward that person. Use a match to melt a bit of the wax on the side of the other candle, and attach your hair to it. This candle represents you as you are now.

Stand in the center of the circle holding both candles carefully so that the hair and coil stay on them. Say, "I bring these two candles between the worlds to represent me and the love I want to draw to me." If a common wick binds them, light the wick in the middle between them and let the first flame of the fire burn them apart. If they're separate, just light them.

As the candles burn, say the emotions that you want to feel while in this relationship. It will feel odd to say them aloud, but it makes the magick powerful. Finally, end by saying "I draw love to me. I am worth loving, and I have love to give. All love is vulnerable and must be protected. Bring me a relationship for our mutual good. So be it." As these candles burn, they release your request and transform it into a reality.

Devoke.

Magickal Wisdom: Magick tends to be about process rather than results.

While you will get results from doing this spell, the resulting girlfriend will be the beginning of a process of continuing in your relationship with her. Although it's masculine in nature, try not to be too goal oriented. Your new relationship is a process of having a partner, not just finding her. Being a good listener is invaluable. You'll notice that women talk a lot about how they feel and that when they talk they're usually not presenting a problem for you to fix. A woman looks for a man who can express the emotions he's feeling. If you accept your emotions, you'll have an easier time expressing your feelings. You don't have to have a problem to express a feeling to your partner. Women are not looking to help you solve your problems; they're looking to be included in your life. Telling your partner how you feel about an issue won't be perceived as whining unless you're complaining about her. But it will strengthen your connection to her. And you'll find that this spell starts that ongoing process.

Spell 60: For Finding True Love

YOU WILL NEED:

   square of cloth
   seeds
   cinnamon
   1 bead or more
   paper
   pen
   needle
   thread

Have you always dreamed of finding your true love like in a fairy tale? Have you longed to become partners with your soul mate? With this spell, you hurl yourself and your true love on a path toward each other. You are asking for that rare type of love in which two souls connect with a bond that is inseparable on many different levels: physical, emotional, intellectual, and spiritual.

For this spell you're going to make a beaded prayer. For hundreds of years people have taken hopes, wishes, dreams, and prayers and bound them in fabric that is decorated with beads. It's a powerful form of magick all over the world. It doesn't matter if you've sewed before or if this is your first time.

As you prepare, think of the qualities you'd like in a partner. Don't focus on a specific person. Focus on a specific kind of person with all the traits that are complementary to yours.

The fabric should be a piece of material at least 3 × 3

inches, but it can be bigger and does not have to be square. You are going to fold it over so that it acts like wrapping paper to hide what you sew in the center. The pattern and texture should convey love in a way that is simultaneously invigorating yet peaceful. Be deliberate about what fabric you choose. It is best if you take an old piece of your clothing and use the material from that, as it will be steeped in your body's energy. The beads should be of materials (for example, wood or glass) and colors that you like and should have energy that you want to draw to you. Any seeds are fine, but it's best to use ones from your favorite fruit or flower.

The Spell: Ground and center. Cast the circle.

Sit down in the center of the circle and take a deep breath. Feel calmness, and connect with your heart by trying to feel its warmth and by being conscious of its beating rhythm. When you are connected to your heart, begin to imagine the traits that you want in a life partner. Think about the deep love that you want to feel. But also think of the traits that make someone easy to live with day by day. Think of someone gentle, appreciative, and funny. Think of someone who smiles and laughs. Think of someone who shares, listens, and communicates with you. As you do this, write the qualities you visualize on the piece of paper. Write that you want to be the best partner you can for this person. Fold it in half once, and put the seeds in the fold. Fold it in half a second time, and sprinkle the cinnamon in that fold. Fold it a third time.

Pick up your piece of fabric, fold it over, and put the piece of paper in it. Begin to sew it into the shape that you'd like as long as the folded paper within is completely hidden. As you sew, chant, "Love is the law, love under will."

Decorate the fabric with at least one bead or many more if you like. As you sew on each bead, say, "I shorten the distance between my true love and me. May we come to meet at the soonest opportunity that will support our relationship and will allow us to grow close."

When you are done creating the beaded prayer, stand in the center and hold it with both hands cupping it. Say, "I call my true love to me. May I be the best partner possible for this person. May this person be the best partner possible for me. May we both live in love, health, and happiness. So mote it be." Put the beaded prayer on your altar.

Devoke.

Magickal Wisdom: Major transformation takes time to manifest.

While it's possible that your true love will show up on your doorstep the day after you do this spell, it's much more probable that this spell will take some time to do its work. Think of how many obstructions must be removed to clear the path for the two of you to meet, fall in love, recognize that you've found each other, and commit to each other. This spell will begin to change you so that you're ready for your true love and your partner can recognize you. And he or she will also begin to change to be the right partner for you, although he or she may not be doing magick to hasten the process. So be patient after doing this spell. It's working. But it's the type of spell that's doing a huge task, the sort that takes multiple major changes to happen. The good thing is that once you've done the spell, you and your beloved have started on the path toward each other as quickly as possible.

Adeptitude

You have finished the spells in this book, and I suspect you aren't only able to access your intuition, you know to value it and act on its guidance. This means that when you go between the worlds, your magick magnifies. While you haven't cast all the spells, you have gained the wisdom presented with each one along the way, and this is far more important for your spellcraft.

The spells in this chapter have continued the process of developing the beauty within you, such as in finding the right outfit. But the spells here also guide you to romantic connections that are both light and fun, as in the passionate kiss spell or heading toward more lasting relationships as in the boyfriend, girlfriend, and true love spells. With these spells you are ready to live a fully magickal life.

What is the key to leading a magickal life? You can change your mind. The entire process in this book has helped you to change your mind so that you can change your life. Changing focus, putting your mind in a point of view, will change how you interpret what you see and how you act. When you view the world as a place full of magick, you will be able to work with that web of energy.

What is the key to living a magickal life?

Changing your mind. **The ability to change your mind is the key to living a magickal life.**

Magick may not take you exactly where you expect it to go, but if you follow the lead given to you by the spiritual realms, you will go further than your expectations in getting what you want throughout your life.

THE ADEPT SPELLCASTER—
ALCHEMY

CONGRATULATIONS! You've made it through all these spells. Perhaps you started out wanting to find out what magick was and to cast a few spells. But what you've really done is to go through a whole training course in magick. That's a big accomplishment. You have a new understanding of the world and of how energy connects all things in a web. You know that when you focus your mind, body, and spirit, you can cause changes in the world by casting spells. And while it would be hard to explain to someone else, by now you realize that magick is real.

While gaining your new skills, you have probably also changed your outlook on life. You can see that by changing the way you act in a situation, you can change how the people around you act. And not just people, but animals, plants, and objects. You can get people to understand you better, and you can express yourself better. And if something is not going right, you can change it. This is the gold you created. You have become an alchemist by being able to change yourself and your situation. You are directing your life as you want it to be.

Magick is about changing your mind and your life path. The more magick you work, the more you reroute the wiring in your brain to make your magick precise and effective. In all honesty, this is something that only you can do for yourself. I can offer you some spells, but I cannot make your brain have the correct mindset for the spell to work. This is true of doctors and psychiatrists as well. If you break a bone, your doctor will set it to heal. But it is your body that does the healing. The doctor just set it on the right course. If you go to a psychiatrist for therapy, the psychiatrist will make suggestions for new behaviors and perhaps augment the treatment with medicine, but the patient is the one who makes up his or her mind to change and adopts the new behavior patterns in life. The same is true of magick. You can find out about the spirit world by reading what others say, but you will not lead a magickal life until you experience magick yourself.

And now you are ready to continue your exploration of the magickal realms. As you work with energy, magick will naturally send you on a path of personal growth. You will become a better person. Only you can rise to meet the challenges of your own magickal path.

MAGICKAL WISDOM

Topics by Spell

Spell 1: For Keeping One's Room Private
Magickal Wisdom: Casting a circle creates a sacred, protected space.

Spell 2: For Consecrating Your Book of Shadows
Magickal Wisdom: A book of shadows is a magickal tool.

Spell 3: For Setting Up Your Altar
Magickal Wisdom: Everyone recognizes magick uniquely.

Spell 4: For Hallowing a Garment
Magickal Wisdom: Restrict magickal items for magickal use.

Spell 5: For Calling Your Athame to You
Magickal Wisdom: Everything has a spirit.

Spell 6: For Finding Your Wand
Magickal Wisdom: Trust your intuition.

Spell 7: For Encountering Your Cup
Magickal Wisdom: An ordinary item can be magickal.

Spell 8: For Gathering Materials for Spells
Magickal Wisdom: Magickal gifts come in unexpected ways and places.

Spell 9: For Creating a Good Luck Talisman
Magickal Wisdom: Visualization is more than imagination.

Spell 10: For Making a Pimple Disappear
Magickal Wisdom: Prepare for spells, and reinforce them with ordinary actions.

Spell 11: Against Acne
Magickal Wisdom: Your subconscious guides you when you
   need it.

Spell 12: Against Weight Problems
Magickal Wisdom: The natural world preserves an order of
   balance.

Spell 13: Against Bad Hair
Magickal Wisdom: Magick prefers that you use the easiest
   method first.

Spell 14: For Diminishing PMS
Magickal Wisdom: Breath is a physical way to focus your
   energy.

Spell 15: Against Cramps
Magickal Wisdom: Exercise improves your ability to move
   energy.

Spell 16: For Increasing One's Own Beauty
Magickal Wisdom: Energy moves through your body best when
   you are properly aligned.

Spell 17: For Keeping a Straight Face
Magickal Wisdom: Magick and drugs do not mix.

Spell 18: For Getting Over a Cold or Flu
Magickal Wisdom: Staying healthy and avoiding stress promote
   effective magick.

Spell 19: For Protection in the Cafeteria
Magickal Wisdom: Harm none.

Spell 20: Against Falling Asleep in Class
Magickal Wisdom: Magick is real.

Spell 21: For Late-Night Energy
Magickal Wisdom: Synchronicity is your magickal tool.

Spell 22: Against Difficult Homework
Magickal Wisdom: Look for patterns in life.

Spell 23: For Protecting Your Computer Files
Magickal Wisdom: A spell can be broken.

Spell 24: For Keeping One's Locker from Being Opened
Magickal Wisdom: Believe; do not doubt.

Spell 25: Against Detention
Magickal Wisdom: Destruction is a valid magickal force.

Spell 26: For Eloquent Speaking
Magickal Wisdom: The way you communicate the spell adds
  power to it.

Spell 27: For Tests and Exams in Classes
Magickal Wisdom: Once an item is charged, preserve your
  intention with that item.

Spell 28: For Help Taking SATs and Other Standardized Tests
Magickal Wisdom: Get the timing right.

Spell 29: For Support from a Teacher
Magickal Wisdom: Manipulative magick is bad even if your
  intention is good.

Spell 30: For Aid from a Student
Magickal Wisdom: Accept responsibility for your magick.

Spell 31: For Focus
Magickal Wisdom: Keep your magickal focus.

Spell 32: For Impenetrable Defense
Magickal Wisdom: Focus your spells in the positive.

Spell 33: For Winning
Magickal Wisdom: Together your thoughts and feelings magnify a spell's power.

Spell 34: For Getting a Good Part in the Play
Magickal Wisdom: The universe is out to help you.

Spell 35: For Having an Easy Time While Babysitting
Magickal Wisdom: What you send out comes back to you
intensified.

Spell 36: For Creative Writing
Magickal Wisdom: Be precise with your request.

Spell 37: For Artistic Excellence
Magickal Wisdom: Sleep on it.

Spell 38: For Invoking Demons to Smite Your Enemies
Magickal Wisdom: If you ask for the impossible, magick will
respond with nonsense.

Spell 39: For Sibling Relations
Magickal Wisdom: Avoid manipulative magick by careful planning before casting a spell.

Spell 40: Against Family Discord
Magickal Wisdom: Magick urges you to confront your faults.

Spell 41: For Explaining Difficult Matters to Parents
Magickal Wisdom: Interpretation is a spiritual act.

Spell 42: For Preventing Others from Eating Your Food in the
Fridge
Magickal Wisdom: Every spirit has needs.

Spell 43: For Softening Punishment Before the Punishment Is
Given
Magickal Wisdom: Magick will try to put you in the right place
for your next step.

Spell 44: For Easing a Separation
Magickal Wisdom: Change, even for positive reasons, is stressful.

Spell 45: For Invisibility
Magickal Wisdom: Be conscious of the footprint you leave
behind.

Spell 46: For Attracting a New Friend
Magickal Wisdom: Make sure that you honestly want what you
are asking for.

Spell 47: For Communicating Something Important
Magickal Wisdom: You have an infinite capacity for love.

Spell 48: Against Jealousy
Magickal Wisdom: Plan destructive spells carefully.

Spell 49: For Strength in Your Decisions and Actions
Magickal Wisdom: Figure out who you are and stand for it
spiritually.

Spell 50: Against Gossip
Magickal Wisdom: Avoid baneful and brat magick.

Spell 51: For Helping a Friend
Magickal Wisdom: Be a giver as well as taker.

Spell 52: For Staying Connected to a Friend While You Are
Apart
Magickal Wisdom: Magick does not know distance.

Spell 53: For Sealing True Friendship
Magickal Wisdom: Honor the magickal within the mundane.

Spell 54: For Finding the Right Outfit
Magickal Wisdom: Personal investment makes someone most
qualified to cast a spell.

Spell 55: For Receiving a Passionate Kiss
Magickal Wisdom: A kiss blends magickal energy.

Spell 56: To Become a Soulful Kisser
Magickal Wisdom: Personal transformation is high magick.

Spell 57: For Getting a Date
Magickal Wisdom: Time is elastic.

Spell 58: For Attracting a Boyfriend
Magickal Wisdom: Love rewards those who can stand alone
before those who cannot.

Spell 59: For Attracting a Girlfriend
Magickal Wisdom: Magick tends to be about process rather
than results.

Spell 60: For Finding True Love
Magickal Wisdom: Major transformation takes time to manifest.

B⊕⊕KS ⊕F INTEREST

Charm Spells: White Magic for Love and Friendship, School and Home by Ileana Abrev, Conari Press, 2004.

Earth, Air, Fire and Water: More Techniques of Natural Magick by Scott Cunningham, Llewellyn Publications, 1991.

Earth Power: Techniques of Natural Magic by Scott Cunningham, Llewellyn Publications, 1983.

Elements of Witchcraft: Natural Magick for Teens by Ellen Dugan, Llewellyn Publications, 2003.

The Girls' Handbook of Spells: Charm Your Way to Popularity and Power! by Antonia Beattie, Prentice Hall Press, 2001.

Living Wicca by Scott Cunningham, Llewellyn Publications, 1993.

Seasons of Magic: A Girl's Journey by Laurel Ann Reinhardt, Llewellyn Publications, 2001.

The Second Circle: Tools for the Advancing Pagan by Venecia Rauls, Citadel Press, 2004.

Spellcraft for Teens: A Magickal Guide to Writing and Casting Spells by Gwinevere Rain, Llewellyn Publications, 2002.

Spell Crafts by Scott Cunningham and David Harrington, Llewellyn Publications, 1993.

Spells for Teenage Witches: Get Your Way with Magical Power by Marina Baker, Seastone, 2000.

Star Power: Astrology for Teens by Rob MacGregor and Megan MacGregor, New Page Books, 2003.

The Teen Book of Shadows: Star Signs, Spells, Potions, and Powers by Patricia Telesco, Citadel, 2004.

The Teen Spell Book: Magick for Young Witches by Jamie Wood, Celestial Arts, 2001.

21st Century Wicca: A Young Witch's Guide to Living the Magical Life by Jennifer Hunter, Citadel Press, 1997.

Where to Park Your Broomstick: A Teen's Guide to Witchcraft by Lauren Manoy, Fireside, 2002.

Who Are You? 101 Ways of Seeing Yourself by Malcolm Godwin, Penguin Arkana, 2000.

Wicca: A Guide for the Solitary Practitioner by Scott Cunningham, Llewellyn Publications, 1988.

Your Book of Shadows: How to Write Your Own Magickal Spells by Patricia Telesco, Citadel, 1999.

PAGAN WEBSITES

The following is a list of websites with information, resources, and links about spells, magick, and spirituality. Of course, there are many more than this.

www.avatarsearch.com

www.azuregreen.com

www.beliefnet.com

www.celticcrow.com

www.cog.org

www.neopagan.com

www.pagannation.com

www.witchvox.com

PAGAN BOOKSTORES

The following bookstores are some of many where you can get magickal books and supplies. Bookstores often host terrific events and are a great place to meet like-minded people.

The Broom Closet
3 Central Street
Salem, MA 01970
(978) 741-3669
www.broomcloset.com

Crone's Cupboard Magick
712 North Orchard Road
Boise, ID 83706
(208) 333-0831
www.crones-cupboard.com

The Enchanted Willow
   Alchemy Shoppe
418 SW 6th Avenue
Topeka, KS 66603
(785) 235-3776
www.enchantedwillow.com

Enchantments
341 East 9th Street
New York, NY 10003
(212) 228-4394
www.enchantmentsincnyc.
   com/our_retail_store.htm

House of Magick
1210 E. Oklahoma Avenue
Milwaukee, WI 53207
(414) 294-3444
www.houseofmagick.com

Magickal Realms
2486 Webster Avenue
Bronx, NY 10458
(718) 892-5350
www.magickalrealms.com

Mystickal Tymes
127 South Main Street
New Hope, PA 18938
(215) 862-5629
www.mystickaltymes.com

Panpipes Magickal
   Marketplace
1641 N. Cahuenga Boulevard
Hollywood, CA 90028
(323) 462-7078
www.panpipes.com

Purple Moon
45 Pandanaram Road
Danbury, CT 06811
(203) 730-2412

Pyramid Books
214 Derby Street
Salem, MA 01970
(978) 745-7171
www.salemctr.com/pyramid.
 html

Quantum Alchemy
913 Corona Street
Denver, CO 80218
(303) 863-0548
www.quantumalchemy.com

Salem West
1209 North High Street
Columbus, OH 43201
(614) 421-7557

Three Sisters Bookstore
866 Main Street
Sanford, ME
(207) 324-1100
www.threesistersbookstore.
 com

ABOUT THE AUTHOR

ALYRA has been a practicing witch since 1987. She has attended numerous pagan gatherings and lives in New York. She can be reached by e-mail at alyra@archermagick. com. Visit her online at www.archermagick.com for free spells, information about magick, links, and other resources.